Can we Talk

and other stories

Published by Weaver Press, Box A1922, Avondale, Harare. 2017
<www.weaverpresszimbabwe.com>

First published by Baobab Books, Harare, 1998, reprinted 2001

© Shimmer Chinodya, 2017

© Photograph of Shimmer Chinodya, Weaver Press,
Typeset by Weaver Press
Cover Design: Harare.
Printed by: Rocking Rat, Harare.

ISBN: 978-1-77922-315-9

Can we Talk
and other stories

by

Shimmer Chinodya

Shimmer Chinodya was born in 1957 in Gweru, the second child in a large, happy family. He studied English Literature and Education at the University of Zimbabwe. After a spell teaching and with curriculum development, he earned an MA in Creative Writing the Iowa Writers' Workshop (USA).

His first novel, *Dew in the Morning*, was published in 1982. This was followed by *Farai's Girls* (1984), *Child of War* (under the pen name B.Chirasha, 1986), *Harvest of Thorns* (1989), *Can We Talk and other stories* (1998), *Tale of Tamari* (2004), *Chairman of Fools* (2005), *Strife* (2006), *Tindo's Quest* (2011), *Chioniso and other stories* (2012) and *Harvest of Thorns Classic: A Play* (2016). His work appears in numerous anthologies. He has also written educational texts, training manuals, radio and film scripts, including the script for the feature film, *Everyone's Child*. He has won many awards for his work, including the Commonwealth Writers Prize (Africa Region) for *Harvest of Thorns*, a Caine Prize shortlist for *Can we Talk* and the NOMA award for publishing in Africa for *Strife*. He has won awards on many occasions from ZIWU, ZBPA and NAMA. He has also received many fellowships abroad and from 1995 to 1997 was Distinguished Dana Professor in Creative Writing and African Literature at the University of St Lawrence in upstate New York.

Contents

Hoffman Street

Our house was blue. It was near the end of the street. At the front there were banana trees and sugar-cane. At night the bananas shivered and shook.

There were ghosts in the bananas. I dreamt about the ghosts. One of the ghosts had a sword. One night the ghost stabbed me with his sword and I died. Then I woke up. Mother was lighting the candle. She gave me a cup of tea and a scone. Then she said, 'Go back to sleep.'

After supper we went to wash the dishes. The ghosts were waiting for us. One of them had a white helmet. Two of them went into the bathroom. The bathroom was where the tap was. We shared the bathroom with the next doors. We hid near the wall waiting for Rhakeri. Rhakeri was the girl next door. She wasn't little. She was not afraid of ghosts. We heard Rhakeri's footsteps. We heard her singing. We heard her opening the tap. Then we rushed out with our plates. We put the plates under the running tap. Rhakeri let us do that. One night mother said, `So, Rhakeri is your mother!'

Rhakeri was nice. She wasn't little. Sometimes we peeped at her when she was taking a shower. The bathroom door had cracks. It wasn't nice of us to do that. But Rhakeri didn't know. One day she caught us peeping and she said, '*Imi! Imi! Ibvai! Ibvai!*'* One day she picked up a purse full of money. She brought the purse home to her mother. Her mother showed my mother the purse. Her mother said, 'What shall I do?' Mother said, 'Take it to the police.' And Rhakeri's mother said, 'Rhakeri!'

Dorothy was little. Dorothy was Rhakeri's sister. Dorothy was my wife. We had two babies – a boy and a girl. Dorothy baked scones on a banana leaf and said, 'Tea is ready.' She washed my clothes in a plate and said, 'Go to work.' When I came back from work I brought her fish and cakes and bananas and she said, 'Come into the bedroom.' Sometimes she made a horrible noise and shook a piece of paper in my face. It wasn't nice to do that. But I liked her. One day mother caught me with Dorothy. We were in a blanket. We wanted to have another baby. Mother beat me with a stick. But Dorothy's mother only laughed and laughed and laughed.

Every night I wet the blankets. I tried and tried and tried. But it was no good. Father woke us up three times a night. But it was no good. Father said to me, 'You are the Kariba Dam.' Rindai was bad too. Father said to him, 'You are the Zambezi River.' But Kelvin was the worst. Father said to him. 'You are the Indian Ocean.' I said to Rindai. 'Who is Kariba?' But Rindai only laughed and laughed. Rindai was going to school. Rindai sat on the sofa reading the newspaper to father. Rindai turned the knob on the radio. Rindai took the cover out of the back of the radio and said. 'This is my ruler.' I wasn't going to school but I could count. I wasn't going to school but I could write my name. I said to father. 'When can I go to school?' and he said, 'When you stop wetting the blankets.' Every night I tried to stop wetting the bed. But it was no good. I said, 'When I grow up I want to be a teacher.' So I said to Dorothy, 'One plus one.' She said, 'Three.' She was very silly. She made a horrible noise and shook a banana leaf in my face. I hit her with a stick. I said to Kuda, 'Write down your name.' Kuda scribbled in the dust with his toe. I hit him with the stick. I said to Joyce, 'Spelling *teacher!*' But she tried to run away. I hit her with the stick.

---

* 'You there! Get away! Get away!'

I wanted to be a teacher. But sometimes I wanted to be a builder. On Sundays after church I wanted to be a builder. I played with bricks. They were building our church. There were no windows on the church. There was no roof. The deacon said to me, 'You are a good builder,' I liked that. He was very nice to say that. I said, 'I want to be an ice-cream man.' The deacon said, 'Why?' I said, 'So that I can eat all the ice-cream myself.' The deacon leaughed and laughed.

We usually ate sadza and vegetables. Every night I dreamt of fish and cakes and bananas. Mother liked fish. Sometimes she cooked a big fat fish. Father and mother sat at the table. We sat on the floor. We ate from the same plate. Father threw pieces of fish onto our plate. Sometimes father threw slices of bread onto our plate. Mother said, 'If you swallow a fishbone you will die.' One day I swallowed a fishbone. I felt it sticking in my throat. I started to die. Father pushed a ball of sadza down my throat and said, 'Don't do it again!' I liked fish and cakes and bananas. But meat-pies were very nice. Because of their smell. And sausages were very very nice. Joyce's mother always made sausages. I went behind the house to smell them. Joyce's mother's house was not far away. It was next to Rhakeri's. Sometimes Joyce came over with a piece of sausage and gave me a bite. So when I said 'Spelling *teacher*!' I did not hit her with the stick. Joyce's mother was very beautiful,. She smelt nice. But when you said, 'Good morning, Mai Joyce,' she did not reply. Joyce's father put on gumboots. He watered the flowers with a hosepipe. He always whistled to himself. Sometimes father sent Rindai and me to borrow the hosepipe. Joyce's father said, 'Well all right. But don't twist the mouth.' One day Rhakeri said to Rindai, 'Joyce's father is not Joyce's father.' I said to Rhakeri, 'What did you say?' and Rhakeri said, '*Iwe! Iwe!* Shut up!'

A big fat man sometimes visited Mai Joyce's house. Then there would be sausages and chicken cooking. Then the big man came out of the house. There were other people with him. Joyce's father was with them. Some of them wore hats made of animal skins. The big man lifted his hand and said, 'We'll take this country.' I said to Rindai 'What's a country?' and he said, 'So where do you think you live?'

Sometimes Sekuru VemaOrange came by. He rode an order bicycle and said, 'Hellow *dana!*' to the children. He took out a bunch of bananas and said, 'Here *dana!*' Sometimes he came into our house and told us stories. Once upon a time Baboon and Hare said, 'Let's cook each other.' First, Baboon cooked Hare. Hare said, 'I'm burning! I'm burning!' And Baboon took Hare out of the pot. Then Hare cooked Baboon. Baboon said, 'I'm burning! I'm burning!' Hare said, 'Burn! Burn!' And Hare ate Baboon. Hare sucked Baboon's bones and started singing:

Perere gumpe sas'pekana
Ntelecha wafa haiwa perere gumpe
Perere gumpe sas'pekana
Ntelecha wafa haiwa perere gumpe[†]

Sekuru VemaOrange had large ears and long teeth. He had long hairs all over his face. There were hairs hiding on his chest, under his overalls. He looked like Baboon. He told us many stories. After a story he said, 'Spelling *chin'apandhle!* Rindai tried and tried and tried. But it was no good. Sekuru VemaOrange never hit us with a stick. He gave us an orange each and said, 'Bye-bye *dana!*' We never visited him. He lived from place to place. Father said. 'Get a house, Sekuru.'

Vatete Mai Farai was nice too. She worked in a white woman's house. She rode a Humber bicycle. She always said, 'Madam said ... Madam said.'

Sometimes her dress got caught in the chain of her bicycle. She stopped and said, 'Take it out for me.' She lived in the other street. She said '*Bhudhi*' to my father. She said to my mother, '*Mukadzi wehazvanzi yangu.*'[‡] She brought us cakes and said, '*Idyai, Vana vehazvanzi yangu*'[§] She said to me, 'I was there when you were born.' She said, 'You gave your mother trouble.'

Baba Keni was not so nice. His house was opposite ours. Every night he came back from the beer hall and started shouting. He did

---

[†]   *Perere gumpe*, we were cooking each other
Baboon is dead, *haiwa perere gumpe*
Perere gumpe, we were cooking each other
Baboon is dead, *haiwa perere gumpe*
[‡]   Sister-in-law (i.e. wife of my brother).
[§]   Eat! Children of my brother.'

4

not want people stepping in his yard. Rhakeri said, 'Baba Keni's head is not all right.' I said, 'What did you say?' Rindai said *'Iwe! Iwe! Shut up!'* I said to myself, 'When I grow up I will not drink beer.' But there was a big mulberry tree in Baba Keni's yard. All the children came to eat the mulberries. Baba Keni said, 'Eat! Eat! *Demet wenyu!'* Mai Keni shook her head and said, 'Just be sure to sweep my yard!' Kuda climbed the tree to shake down the mulberries. He was a good climber. I was afraid to climb trees. Mother said, 'If you climb trees you will break your neck and die.'

Next door was Jeremiah's family. They were on the other side. Jeremiah's father cut the children's hair. He was very smart. He used a pair of scissors. Father said, 'Here is a tickey. Get your hair cut.' Jeremiah's father said, 'Did you oil your hair?' Jeremiah's father whistled as he cut my hair. He said to me, 'Your skin is very smooth. You're going to be a big brain.' I said to Rindai, 'What's a big brain?' Rindai said, 'Who told you that?' and I said, 'Jeremiah's father'. Sometimes Jeremiah gave me big fat guavas on a plate. Jeremiah always winked when he did something nice. Mother said, 'Did you say thank you to Jeremiah?' I never hit Jeremiah with the stick. Because I wanted the guavas. And Jeremiah knew one plus one. He knew 'Spelling teacher!'

Sekuru Vekupenda was nice. He lived at the end of the street. He rode a Rudge bicycle. The spokes went 'ts-ts-ts-ts' like somebody spitting. He painted people's houses. When he came to paint our house we took all the things out and played on the lawn. He put on his hat and said, 'Don't touch the walls till they are dry.' His house was painted pink.

Babamunini Masamba lived next to Baba Jeremiah. He had a huge scar on his hand. He worked in a butchery in town. He rode his bicycle very fast. He rang the bell for the children. He always carried a packet of meat home. His wife was very quiet. I liked to be sent to their house. Mainini Masamba put a bowl of meat in front of me and I ate. I got home and mother said, 'Did you eat anything there?' and I said, 'I don't know' and she said, 'Don't eat in people's houses,' and I said, 'Well, all right.' Babamunini Masamba went to our church. One day he was preaching. He showed people the scar on his hand.

He said, 'I got nothing. I got nothing. Colourbar. Colourbar.' I said to Rindai, 'Who is Colourbar?' and he said, 'Schupet! It's something with two colours.'

One day Spoo and Roger said to us, 'You are not the Four Dragons!' Spoo and Roger lived next to Baba Keni. Rindai said, 'Yes, we're the Four Dragons.' Spoo said, 'No, you're not.' Rindai said to Kelvin and me, 'Let's be the Four Dragons.' We took the pots and the spoons. We started beating the pots with the spoons. We started beating the pots with the spoons. We started singing. It was a Thursday afternoon. Mother had gone to church. The women started coming back from church. They were wearing uniforms. White and black uniforms. Purple uniforms. Maroon uniforms. Blue uniforms. Methodist uniforms. Adventist uniforms. Kelvin said, 'Oh, there's mother!' Mother exclaimed, 'What are you doing with my pots and pans?' Kelvin said, 'We are the Four Dragons.' Mother said, 'Wait till your father comes back.' Father came back. He stood his bicycle against the wall. We hid in the spare room. Father said, 'Get out boys! Out, out boys!' He said that when we did something wrong. We went out to the bananas. It was getting dark. It was very cold. Very very cold. In the sky the clouds were all running away from the moon. The cold was chasing away the clouds. I heard the ghosts shivering in the bananas. The one with the white helmet said, 'Today you will die.' I closed my eyes and waited to die. Then we heard Rhakeri's footsteps. She was going to the tap. We called out but she was too far away. We stayed in the bananas for a very long time. Then the door opened and mother said, 'Please let them in now.' Father said, 'Come in boys!' Father said, 'Give them some warm tea and scones.' The radio said, 'Here is the seven o'clock news.' Then father said, 'Let us pray.'

Enias was Rhakeri's big brother. He had a beard on his face. He was as tall as the bathroom door. Sometimes he stayed and sometimes he did not. One day he lifted me and put me on the roof. I could see all the other roofs. I said, 'Eniasi Enias! Take me down!' He went away. I could see all the other roofs. There were roofs everywhere. Roofs roofs everywhere. Some of the roofs had things on them. I couldn't see houses. I couldn't see people. I started to cry. Then Enias came back. He said, 'Well, all right.' He put me down on the lawn. He took off his shoe. He said, 'Eat my big toe.' I said, 'Please, Enias.' He said, 'Eat my toe. Or I will dig a big hole and cover you up.' I put my face to his toe. He did not smell very nice. Then he said, 'Here is a tickey. You can go now.' And he laughed and laughed and laughed.

One day there was red soil in the bathroom in the morning. Mother said, 'Don't go there.' But I ran out and looked. Rhakeri's mother came over. She looked very sad. She said to my mother, 'Enias dug up somebody.' She said, 'They'll lock him up.' I said to Dorothy, 'Your brother dug up somebody.' She said, 'No he did not.' I said, 'I won't play with you.' I did not talk to Dorothy for a long time. Perhaps the whole day. But Dorothy came over with two toffees. I said, 'Can I have one?' and she gave it to me.

I got sick. It was Dorothy's toffee. It was the red soil in the bathroom. I was going to die. Then Enias would dig me up. Mother said, 'What's wrong?' and I said, 'It's my feet.' Father said, 'What's wrong?' and I said, 'It's my head.' Father said, 'Make him some warm tea and scones.' Kelvin wanted to eat the scones. I said to Kelvin, 'But you are not sick.' I sat in the spare room. It was very cold in the house. Outside the the sun was shining. But I did not go out. Because I was very sick. Father brought meat pie. He said 'What's wrong now?' I said, 'It's my shoulders.' Kelvin wanted to eat the meat pie. I said to him, 'But you are not sick.' And he said, 'Now I'm sick,' and I said, 'But you are not sick.'

Mother said to me, 'Now you are a bad boy. Now Jesus will make you really sick.' So I said, 'Sorry sorry Jesus.' But I woke up shouting. Enias was putting me on the roof. Enias was digging me up. Father put a hand on my forehead and said, 'Go back to sleep.' Next morning mother took me to the clinic. There were lots of other children. They were all sick. They all wanted to die. Then Enias would put them on the roofs. Then Enias would dig them up. But their fathers would give them meat-pies first. The nurse put a hand on my forehead. I knew the nurse. One day she came to our house and I said, 'Nurse, nurse, there are pumpkins cooking in the pot' and she laughed and laughed. The nurse put her hand on my forehead and said, 'Don't be sick now.'

She said, 'Please don't be sick.' I said, 'Well, all right.'

Then mother got sick. She did not want to eat. She said, No salt, please.' She said, 'It's my feet.' Rhakeri said, 'Your mother and father did something.' I said to Rindai, 'What did mother and father do?' Rindai said, `lwe! Lwe! Shut up.' Father bought mother fish. Mother said, 'No fish, please.' Father brought mother apples! Mother said, 'No apples, please.' Father brought mother peas. Mother said, 'No peas, please.' But mother was getting fat. I said to Rindai, 'Why is mother getting fatter and fatter?' Rindai laughed and laughed. Then mother went away. Vatete Mai Farai came and cooked. I said, 'Vatete, Vatete, where is mother?' Vatete said, 'She'll come soon.' I was afraid mother would die. Then Enias would dig her up. But mother was too fat. Enias could not put her on the roof. Enias could not dig her up. Then mother came back. She came back in a green car. She was carrying something in a white blanket. Vatete said, 'Look, look. The baby looks like you.' I touched the little face. The little face was red as blood. Mai Keni came to see the baby. Mai Kuda came to see the baby. Mai Jeremiah came to see the baby. But Mai Joyce did not come. Vatete said to mother, 'Don't let Mai Rhakeri come. Don't let that woman near your baby.' But Mai Rhakeri came. She came and sat on the bed and said, 'Oh, what a pretty girl.' Sometimes the baby cried. Sometimes the baby did not. Sometimes Rhakeri and Rindai sat on the floor and held the baby. Rhakeri brought a pair of booties for the baby. 'I picked up some money,' she said. 'I bought these for the baby.' Thank you, Rhakeri,' mother said. Then mother said to Kelvin and Dorothy and me, 'You're too small to hold the baby.' Then we went out to play.

The Man who Hanged Himself

One day Bhudhi Edwin came back from the Matroko Bush where he had gone to get himself a chewing stick and he said, 'There's a man who's hanged himself in a tree near the rail-trucks.'

It was a warm November Sunday morning and we were polishing shoes, getting ready to go to church. I put down down Daddy's fat, black, bunshaped Size 10s and squinted into the sun.

'He's squatting on the anthill between the *pafa* trees with his head thrown back right over his shoulder,' Bhudhi Edwin said, digging at his gums and spitting out bits of stick.

'He strung the rope to a tree branch and slid down the trunk to the ground. Must've done it just before sunrise.'

'Have you told the police?' Batsirai gasped.

'Why should I be the one to break the news?' Bhudhi Edwin said, rinsing his mouth at the garden tap.

'Are you going to tell father?' Dzimai asked.

'Now you all shut up,' Bhudhi Edwin said, tossing away his stick and flinging himself to the edge of the lawn. He yanked his stockings right up to his knees, picked up a wire brush and scrubbed his black Tenderfoots. 'If anyone says a word about this to father or mother, I'll give him the best of my Size 8s.'

'So, did you touch him, Bhudhi Edwin?' Dzimai continued, un-daunted by the prospect of a boot up his bum.

'Me, touch him! You don't touch things like that unless you want them following you into your house.'

'But why would he do that to himself?' said Batsirai.

'Don't ask me!'

I looked out towards Matroko Bush: an area of scrub, of squatting thorn trees, acacias and criss-crossing footpaths. It began at the edge of the township, perhaps six or seven hundred metres from our house. A man zipped out of the trees on a bike. After a while, a couple came down the dust road skirting the western end of the township and leisurely ambled into the trees.

'Are you sure the man wasn't just kneeling on the ground, Bhudhi Edwin?' I said.

'Idiot!' He kicked me on the shin. 'Do you think I was born yesterday?'

'Maybe his enemies did it to him, or perhaps some thugs – and just left him there,' Batsirai murmured.

Father came out with his raincoat, his bibles and hymn books and headed for Matroko Bush. The priest was out on a parish visit and father had been 'given the plan' and would deliver the sermon that afternoon. He liked the cool and the shade and the quiet of the bush when he had a service to prepare, or when he was doing his homework for the night school or writing up the family budget for the month. We all knew he would be writing his Standard Six examinations soon. I felt a pang of alarm as father passed us and strode confidently out to the bush, but Bhudhi Edwin eyed us severely with a look that told us to shut up and we said nothing.

'Hurry up and finish the shoes,' Bhudhi Edwin barked. I plucked my eyes away from Matroko Bush and reached for mother's blue Size 6 *mariposa*.

Some two hours later, after we were bathed and almost dressed for church, father returned from Matroko Bush. He looked serious, his face frowning darkly with foreboding, About time too, I thought.

'All you boys, come into the house,' he said.

I looked expectantly up at Bhudhi Edwin, only got another kick on the shin and shuffled after the others into the house, through the kitchen where mother was mashing the potatoes and fixing the gravy on the old Dover. Shuvai was taking out the plates and the other girls were obliviously playing with their dolls on the floor. We filed into the sitting room and flopped to the floor in front of him, our knees drawn up to our chins.

'Switch off the radio, Edwin,' father commanded. Bhudhi Edwin raised himself on one knee, reached over our heads to the old display cabinet and turned off the Marylyn transistor. Father picked up the exercise book lying on his lap and held it up to our faces, tilted so that we could see its emaciated girth.

'Which of you has been tearing pages out of my night-school books?' he demanded. Silence. We exchanged quick, half guilty, half accusing looks. Silence. Then followed a sermon about the importance of exercise books, of homework, of economics and respect for the property of elders left lying within the reach of little hands, and of the wages of theft. This grievance was apparently a communal crime not worthy of a detailed witch hunt and, perhaps because of father's pious commitments for the day, the matter was dropped with a relatively light reprimand.

'And you Edwin, you're a big boy now and ought to make sure this sort of thing doesn't happen. I expect you to set an example to the others. If this happens again you'll all get a taste of my cane, one that's long overdue, never mind who's done it. Out, now, all of you!'

We trooped back through the kitchen, and out to the yard.

'I didn't do it, you know I can't write yet...' Dzimai swore.

'But I thought father wanted to tell us about the dead man,' Batsirai blurted.

'What dead man?' mother snapped, her face sweaty with the aromatic steam of the potatoes, but we were already out of the kitchen, among the bananas, safely out of earshot.

'Idiots, all of you,' Bhudhi Edwin swore, swinging savagely at our shins.

***

I did not enjoy lunch. I chewed the meat and thought of the man

11

who'd hanged himself.

All through the church service, I thought of the dead man. Father preached an exciting sermon about Legion and the thousand spirits that had tortured him, but I couldn't concentrate. I kept thinking of the man who'd hanged himself. Perhaps he'd been tortured too... but what a thing to do! Put a rope round your neck and slide down a tree trunk and – yank! end your life. Perhaps his wife had run away from him, or his boss had been too hard on him. Or perhaps his children had died one by one, of a strange illness. Perhaps it had all got too much for him. Had anybody found him yet? When would the outcry be raised? Or had the police been and removed his body already? Did he have a family and what would they say? And where was he now – where was the spirit of the dead man? Did he have to wait in a queue for judgement day or had God already said to him, 'You have committed the worst sin in the book and there shall be no trial for you! Get out of my sight!' Had he then stumbled blindly towards Gehena and plunged over into the pits? Was he already sizzling and roasting In a gigantic lick of fire and brimstone and calling out for Lazarus to bring him a drop of water?

Later that afternoon, after we'd returned from church, Bhudhi Edwin went away on father's bicycle. He did not say where he was going – perhaps to see a friend. I realise now that at the age of eighteen and having just scratched through Standard Six, sprouting pimples and a faint moustache and waiting for a job to come up, our cousin was entering that itchy stage where there had to be a girlfriend somewhere. Yes, there had been a letter or two for him and it was possible the missing sheets from father's night-school books had been converted into one of those fervent missives I had spotted in his khakis:

Greenland of Love
P. O. Box Sugar Thighs
Marry Me Soon
Dear my bestest Darling Mobi Moreblessings
(Showers)...

Lalely he did not go bird-shooting or *pafa*-picking with us in the Matroko Bush. He suddenly wanted to be alone. He seemed restless. There were evenings when he'd come back wearing a strange necklace or a bangle, and even carrying a whiff of perfume that rode subtly over his rough breeze of carbolic soap, Shell grease and adolescent sweat, and mother had quietly said to him, 'Good evening, Edwin,' and let him in. Then, even his Size 8 Tenderfoots had relented a little towards our shins. After two years with us in the township, his country-bumpkin manners were being slowly smoothed away.

Today I hoped it was not Miss Sugar Thighs he was cycling off to see. This was no time for frivolity, with that dead man squatting out there on the anthill between the *pafa* trees with his head thrown back over his shoulder and the rope stretching tightly up to the sky, into the tree. A dead man in a bush barely half a mile from our house and on a Sunday, too. I desperately hoped Bhudhi Edwin was going to Matroko Bush to check on the scene, to see if the body and been discovered and removed, or, if it was still there. Perhaps it had begun to go bad, ridden by a hive of flies like the bloated, pungent-smelling dead dogs one sometimes found abandoned in Matroko bush.

I heard the bicycle clinking agains the wall and I knew Bhudhi Edwin was back. I ran out and said to him, 'Well...?'

'Well what?' he cut in, dusting down his safari suit and wiping his Tenderfoots on the doormat.

'Is he still there in the bush?' I whispered hoarsely

'Who?'

The dead man.'

'Idiot!' he rapped. 'Did you think I'd be dumb enough go back there?'

I could not sleep. I'd listened eagerly to the voices of the passers-by on the road, listened carefully to the six and eight o'clock news bulletins, listened right up to the epilogue, but there had been no news of the man who'd hanged himself. Perhaps it would be in the newspapers the next day. Then a sudden, vicious thought struck me that perhaps Bhudhi Edwin had had something to do with it. Something to do with that rope and that head thrown back right over the shoulder. Bhudhi Edwin and his stubborn country ways, always spitting at dead cats and striking matchsticks in the dark and mumbling threats to madmen on the streets. Oh no, God help, no. I just hoped that he had not kicked the dead man in the shin with his Tenderfoots, or spat on him to disarm some curse incurred by his having found the body, found him there, planted among the *pafa* trees where we went to find chewing sticks.

Why else, if he had nothing to do with it, had he not told father, or gone to the police? Did he want it to be his secret, so that it would be said that only he saw it but never reported it? Why else, if he hadn't touched it, had he patted his safari suit and pulled up his stockings when he stood the bicycle against the wall?

And now, for a person who'd discovered a man who'd hanged himself, Bhudhi Edwin slept soundly enough – snoring robustly and dribbling at the corner of his mouth. I myself fell asleep slowly and fitfully. I dreamt about the man who'd hanged himself – the rope creaking in the wind and his head and shoulders swaying and his eyes bulging fatly in their sockets. His tongue hanging stiffly out of his mouth.

Something, a hand, was moving slowly down my belly and my side was warm and wet and I yelled and then I realised it was Bhudhi Edwin's hand and that he must have been awake or had just torn out of sleep and was knocking our heads with his knuckles and kicking our shins and dragging us all over the floor.

'Up, up and out, all of you! Damn it, Dzimai, you've done it again!'

'What's wrong, Edwin?' mother's voice, calm with agitation, called out through the thin wall of their bedroom.

'I'm taking them to the toilet,' Bhudhi Edwin said, and he marched us out of the spare room already reeking of urine, naked and sleepy, bumping into the battered sofas and the bicycle, out through the rattling sitting room door, round the stoop to the front, past the bananas shivering in the moonlight, out to the lavatory. I touched my side and realised it was wet and slippery, but not with urine – but I was too sleepy to think about it. As we filed back into the house I stole a glance at Matroko Bush. In the moonlight I could see the crowns of the *pafa* trees clearly outlined against the sky. There was no wind and everything was very still. I rubbed my side and lay down on the floor and pulled my piece of the blanket over my head.

***

In the morning I listened again to the early news and at school I hung back at P.E. time and skimmed through the teacher's newspaper, but there was no news of the man who'd hanged himself. I waited for the headmaster's announcements at assembly and lingered outside the staff room, eavesdropping on the teachers and at breaktime I scouted for and eavesdropped on any likely gatherings of pupils in the school yard – but there was no word of the man who'd hanged himself.

Then, yes!, just before the end of break I saw a police car pull into the school yard and head for the office. Yes, a blue and white police car and it stopped in front of the staff room and two officers stepped out and marched into the headmaster's office. Suddenly I was filled with excitement and fear because I thought any minute now the headmaster would send for my teacher, asking for the little boy in Grade 1a who lived in Hoffman Street whose brother or cousin had seen the man who'd hanged himself between the *pafa* trees in Matroko Bush. I crept towards the office in trepidation, confident that they were looking for me, grateful that they would come for me and it would soon be over, and yet fearful that I would be accused of having played a part in that cruel act, but after only a few minutes the two officers came out and got into their cars and drove away.

I began to feel a deep disappointment, a sense of betrayal and nibbling doubt. The secret knowledge of the man who'd hanged himself hung heavily on me and I wanted to unburden myself by telling it, but to who? Would my teacher believe me? Would the class not laugh?

I sneaked out through the gates behind the toilets and ran down the street towards the edge of the township. I took a circuitous route so that I would avoid our house, where my mother might spot me but as I was coming out of a hedged alley I ran into a man who belonged to our church and he said, 'Hi, boy!' but I leapt away and kept going without looking back. I kept going till I got to the edge of the bush then I slowed down a bit because among the criss-crossing paths there

15

were strings of thorns on the ground and if I wasn't careful I might get stabbed in the heels, or splash into the great big obscene sausages of human deposition littering the grass. Here was where we came to shoot birds with our catapults and to pick up *pafa* and *bubunu*, here was where we fetched our counting sticks for school, and there, in the hedged enclosure was where the Mapostori gathered up into a big, biblical red sea of doekes and shaven heads to worship on Saturday afternoons and if you stood too close to the edge and did not step back quickly enough when the chief prophet charged about spraying the flock with his holy water and the drops hit your forehead and you were not a member of the sect you might go stark raving mad talking in tongues as your demons came gushing through your throat. These flattened bits under the shade of the big trees were where wicked couples nested and we loved to taunt them with our voices and our catapults – it was even said that one of the prophets was caught there with somebody else's wife. And if you were not careful you might trip over a knot of grass somebody had made across the path or you might step onto a twisted bit of cloth into which somebody had tied up a spell to make you mad or cripple you and no matter how hungry you were or how badly you needed money, you should never ever, ever, ever pick up any coins you saw in the bush, for someone could have thrown away their bad luck with the money. There, look through the border of pine trees across the fence or barbed wire, do you see the cemetery beyond? That is where they bury the white people. And this brown path is where a man chased us one evening shouting, '*Bata! Bata!* Catch! Catch!' and Bhudhi Edwin was convinced it was not just some dagga-crazed lunatic out for our necks.

This was our haunt, the Matroko Bush I knew so well and loved and feared and hated but today, now, here, there was no time for such reflection. The man had hanged himself here – in our bush! I felt a sense of outrage. I slowed down again as I approached the *pafa* trees. My heart was beating faster and faster but I knew I mustn't be afraid. There was no body on the anthill between the *pafa* trees and I knew at once they must have taken the body away. I saw marks on the ground where his knees must have rested, two soft bruises in the dust, almost invisible to the eye. I looked up and saw the branch where the rope must have dangled down – they must have cut it down and carried it away, whoever they were who had removed him, but I looked very, very carefully and I saw a tiny, tiny, frayed piece of fabric, of sisal perhaps, fluttering on the bark near the darkish ring where the rope had gripped the wood. Yes, this was where the man had hanged himself all right. This was where the man had hanged himself and now I could go back home with the secret ominous satisfaction that I had at least seen where it had happened. As I was walking around the place I detected a bad smell, then I almost stepped onto a day-old mound of excrement. Stepping back, I spotted the last irrefutable evidence – a set of footprints in the dust, pacing away from the mound, round the two soft marks in the dust and the circle of *pafa* trees and then heading in the unmistakable direction of the township.

Size 8 Tenderfoots.

Going to See Mr B.V.

The day his father sent him to see Mr B.V., he put on his cream-coloured, long-sleeved shirt, his flared grey 'something-else' trousers and his black moccasin shoes. His mother had suggested he put on a tie and insisted on him having a solid lunch; his father had dropped hints about him needing a haircut, but he had quietly decided on a smart but semi-casual look. Now in Form 3, he was learning to get his own way. He compromised by putting a comb in his back pocket and eating a slice of bread, just in case.

It was a hot, dusty afternoon and he soon began to hate himself for sweating. He sniffed his armpits and smelt the perspiration washing away the soap he'd glazed over them after his shower and realised he should have taken the bus to save the long tramp through the bush and the backyards of the industrial sites, to Mr B.V.'s Wholesales. He'd brushed his teeth carefully and, to keep his breath sweet, he'd bought – with the money he could have used for the bus ticket – a packet of Mint Imperials to suck, but now he found himself chomping nervously through the medium-sized box.

Just before he reached the market-place he stopped in front of a shop window and ran his comb through his hair again. He brought out the dab of Vaseline he had rolled up in a twist of khaki paper and smoothed it on his lips; then he noticed the owner of the shop, a tall white man, pointing at him and he ran on. He stooped to wipe his shoes with an old newspaper. The big watch in Main Street said five past two and he thought that Mr B.V. would have returned from lunch, so he crossed over to to the big wholesale shop. He walked past the yard packed with rows of ploughs, scotch-carts, hoes, door frames, bags of timber and cement to the front where the offices were. In the yard there was a man in a green dust-jacket counting stock. The man was his cousin or nephew or something but he did not want to be held up and he walked on as if he had not seen him.

Right behind the wholesalers there was a departmental store where his father worked and this was managed by Mr J.V., Mr B.V.'s younger brother. Once or twice when he and his brothers had gone into the store, their father had taken them to see Mr J.V., a quiet, busy man in his late thirties who looked sideways at you as if you were about to play a trick on him, nodded briefly and went on with his business. Mr B.V. Was much older and fatter than Mr J.V., had a balding head, and talked and laughed with everyone. He spoke Shona and called their father 'Longman', and if you were lucky, he would take a giant packet of Crystal sweets or Choice Assorted Biscuits right off the shelf and thrust them into your unsuspecting hands.

As he approached the office, he saw Mr B.V. through the small window sitting at his desk inspecting some papers. The man looked briefly in his direction. In a sudden panic, he walked on past the door, and down the street before he turned round and made his way back. He patted his pockets to assure himself that the letter his father had given him was still there, then he walked boldly into the shop. He saw men pushing and packing stacks of goods, and a young Indian woman writing at the counter. He walked on and tapped on the door of the office. Mr B.V. looked up and he stepped in cautiously and stood near the door.

'Good afternoon, Sir,' he said.

Mr B.V. looked up, nodded and then turned his papers over quickly.

'My father said you wanted to see me, Sir,' he said, feeling the perspiration welling up In his armpits.

'Who?' Mr B.V. said, rather surprised.

'My father, Sir. Oh, I'm George Mahari, Sir.'

'You're who?'

'George Mahari, Sir. Mr Mahari's son.'

'Longman? You're Longman's son?'

'Yes, Sir,' he said, momentarily taken aback.

'What can I do for you?' Mr B.V. said, squeezing his hands as if he had just applied a lotion to them.

'My father said that you wanted to see me, Sir,' he said; and when Mr B.V. glanced at his papers and squeezed his hands again, he took out the letter from his pocket and put it on the gleaming glass table and said, 'My father asked me to give you this letter, Sir.'

Mr B.V. slit the letter open expertly with a little knife and skimmed through it.

'Longman wrote this?' he said, stretching back in his padded seat.

'Yes, Sir.'

'Wait outside,' said Mr B.V. 'I'll call you.'

As he stepped out of the office a bald-headed man in spectacles and a white dust-coat called to him from the counter.

'Don't you remember me?' said the man, 'I'm an uncle of yours. Gideon Masimbi is my name. Of course you wouldn't know, the way you keep yourselves locked up at home, studying. Your mother has the same totem as me – the elephant – and I regard your father as my in-law. What's your first name?'

'George,' he said.

Uncle Masimbi shook his hand heartily and introduced him to the other workers in the Wholesale. 'This is Mahari's second son,' he said. 'What form are you doing, now?'

'Form 3,' he said.

'You're a big brain, eh?'

'All Mahari's sons are big brains,' said the man he had ignored in the yard who, as it later turned out, was a distant cousin. 'They have no time to play. They're always at home, studying.'

'Mr B.V. said he wanted to see me. I brought him a letter.'

Going to See Mr B.V.

'You boys are doing very well for your father and we're all proud of you. You have realised that books are the only way out for us people and you are sticking to them. Your father has worked all his life to send you boys through school and you should never forget that. Keep up the good work. And I congratulate your father for raising you the right way. So, what brings you here? Did you come to see Baas B.V.?'

'Yes.'

'But you're not looking for a job yet, are you?'

'No,' George said, 'Mr B.V. wanted to see me.'

'Your father asked you to come and see Baas B.V.?' Uncle Masimbi said, with surprise.

'Yes,' George said hesitantly, 'I brought a letter for Mr B.V.'

'A letter. Oh. And has Baas B.V. seen the letter?'

'He read it and said I should wait for him to call me.'

'Very well,' said Uncle Masimbi, arranging some invoices. After a pause he said, 'Your father and I worked together in this Wholesale long before he met your mother and before anybody dreamt of you boys. You can sit here at the counter if you like, or walk around and see what we do every day. Come, Naison, show him around.'

Naison, the distant cousin whom he'd ignored in the yard, showed him round. The place was dark and dusty and hot with the smell of trapped air. The shelves which rose right up to the ceiling were stacked with clothes of all kinds, school uniforms, kitchenware, groceries and other merchandise. There were a dozen or so customers – mostly shop-owners – placing their orders. After a quick tour, George returned to the counter, anxious to make himself visible once Mr B.V. started looking for him, although right now he was talking animatedly to a young Indian couple.

'Baas B.V. seems rather busy today,' Uncle Masimbi said, checking off a big order at the counter. 'You could go and walk around for a while, otherwise you'll exhaust your feet standing in one place.'

Realising that he might be getting in the way, George went out to the verandah and stood leaning against a pillar where he would be visible from the office. The young visitors left and Mr B.V. continued poring over his papers. At one point George saw Mr B.V. eating some-

21

thing from a lunch-box with his bare hands and licking his fingers. Pickled onions perhaps, George thought, remembering the highly spiced foods Mrs J. V. sometimes gave his father to bring home. As he was eating Mr B.V. looked out of his office and crossed eyes with George. George backed off. He was feeling hungry himself and dammit, he should have had his lunch after all. Rushing off on an empty stomach to spend the afternoon loitering on a verandah watching the passers-by was not his idea of fun. And it was hot – he was sweating freely now and was afraid unsightly yellow rings would form under his armpits. He quickly ran to a cafe at the corner of the street and stuffed himself with two scones and a Coke, wiped his teeth with his thumb and returned to his post on the verandah. The office was empty, but he could hear Mr B.V.'s voice from somewhere in the dark recesses of the shop, shouting names and barking commands. A flurry of activity followed. At five minutes to five George stepped out into the open doorway of the Wholesale. Mr B.V. was standing on a ladder in one of the corridors, packing shirts onto the shelves. He had taken off his coat and rolled up his shirt-sleeves, around and below him stood three or four workers, who passed the shirts up to him.

'You can come in now, M'zukuru George,' Uncle Masimbi called out, and he went to stand at the counter. After a while Mr B.V. came down the ladder, rolled down his sleeves and returned to his office. All the customers had gone; it was time to close the shop. Mr B.V. put on his coat and came out to the counter.

'But why does Longman do this?' Mr B.V. said, holding out the letter and looking first at George and then at Uncle Masimbi. 'How can Longman do this?'

'Is anything wrong, Baas?' Uncle Masimbi asked. A silence fell in the darkening shop and the workers gathered round the counter.

'Why has your father done this?' Mr B.V. asked George, holding out the letter. '*Hini ndava enaLongman aenza so?*'*

'What is all this about?' Uncle Masimbi asked George, taking off his spectacles which made his eyes seemed older and wrinkled with worry. 'What is this letter Baas B.V. is talking about? What's the

---

* Why does Longman do this?

matter, Baas B.V.?'

'Let him explain himself, Gideon. Can't he talk? What's your name again?'

'George, Sir,' the boy said hoarsely.

'What form you are in at school?'

'Form 3, Sir.'

'So why you not answer questions and look stupid? Is that what you do at school to your teachers?'

'No, Sir.'

'So why your father write this letter? Why he doesn't come here, himself? Your father just write this letter and say, Go to Baas B.V. and get money for your school fees and your uniforms. *Haikona mhani.*'

'Is that manners, Gideon? Look, he's written a list of everything in this letter – shirts, trousers, shoes, socks, bags, maths instruments, school fees and he gives this letter to this boy and doesn't come himself. Eh, Gideon, why you people do this, man?'

'No, Baas B.V.,' Uncle Masimbi said, examining the letter. 'It's just a mistake Baas and Longman has to say sorry. I'll speak to him myself and tell him that Baas B.V. was not happy with the letter. But didn't Longman talk to you about this before writing the letter, Baas?'

'Talk to me, Gideon? You know I talk to you people about it every day. I say to you people, if any of you has a problem, come to me and I'll help you. Didn't I pay for your spectacles, Gideon?'

'Yes, you did, Baas.'

'And you, Taruona, didn't I pay for your father's operation last month?'

'You did, Baas,' Taruona, the short young man in a suit behind George said.

'And each time I do that you write a letter or you come to the office and say, Baas B.V., I need this... or Baas B.V. such and such a problem has happened? Now you Gideon and Longman, you the old *madala* have worked here longer than anyone and I have said to you any trouble with school fees for your children, tell me. Not trouble because of drinking Go-beer! Just because I say so doesn't mean I say Longman, write a letter. You hear that, young man? Go tell your

23

father Baas B.V. says he can't have the money for your fees and your uniforms because he is too proud.'

George's eyes were already full of tears and he took a moment to see Mr B.V. holding the letter out to him.

'You know how long your father has worked for me and my brother?'

'No Sir,' George sobbed.

'Twenty-seven years, now. Longman and Gideon were the first two boys we had here and that time we have small shop at the corner. They worked good and were very good boys. They did not have long hands or long eyes and they kept their jobs. And I sent your father to night school. And then we built this Wholesale. And then the Departmental Store where your father works. Your father tell you all this?'

'No, Baas,' George said, hoping to salvage something by that lie.

'How come your father don't tell you all this? How come you don't ask him? Do you know my brother, Mr. J.V.?'

'The one who manages the store where my father works?' George started.

'How come you say "the one who manages the store where my father works"?' Mr B.V. erupted, his eyes flashing, 'Why don't you just say, "my father's boss"? Are you getting proud too, like your father? You think because you're now in Form 3 you can say, 'the one who manages the store where my father works,' Eh?'

'No, Baas B.V.,' said Uncle Masimbi, 'He's just a child, Baas.'

'How come your father doesn't ask his boss for the money? How come your father keeps coming to me when he now has his own Baas? Look at him, Gideon. He's crying. Why are you crying? Do you cry at school?'

'No, Sir.'

'Do you cry at home?'

'No, Sir.'

'Does your father often beat you?'

'No, Sir.'

'How many times a week he beat you, George? Two, three times?'

'I don't know, Sir.'

'Does your father beat your mother?'

'No, Sir.'

'Does your father make your mother cry at night?' Mr B.V. laughed.

'No, Sir.'

'How many wives your father got?'

'One, Sir,' George choked; alarmed by the question.

'Your father have any children with other women?'

'No, Sir.'

'What you do on Sundays?'

'We go to church, Sir.'

'What your father do on Sundays?'

'He goes to church, too.'

'Does your father drink beer?'

'No, Sir.'

'Is that true, Gideon?'

'Very true, Baas B.V. You know yourself Longman doesn't touch a drop and that he goes to church every Sunday.'

'How many witchdoctors come to your house per month?'

'None, Sir.'

'Your father doesn't have a witchdoctor?'

'No, Sir.'

'What kind of African don't have a witchdoctor? What your mother do when you're sick?'

'We go to the clinic, Sir.'

'How many times you go to the reserves to play drums and drink beer and sing songs for dead people?'

'We don't, Sir.'

'Your father is a good boy. He's been working here nearly thirty years now. He mustn't do this. Well, what do you say Gideon? You think we send his son back and say no or we tell Longman to come here tomorrow and explain why he do this?'

Uncle Masimbi glanced again at the figures on the letter and said, 'I think Longman should come to talk to you himself, Baas.'

'*Haikona, mhani. Haafaniri kuita so.*'' When you go back to school?'

'The day after tomorrow, Sir.'

'All right. I say, let's give him the money' Mr B.V. said. 'We'll give you the money, but your father must come and explain first thing tomorrow.'

Mr B.V. went to one of the offices, rang the cash register and while he was there counting out the money, Uncle Masimbi adjusted his glasses and took another worried glance at the figures on the letter and said in subdued tones, to George, 'Your father really mustn't do this because it makes things too hard for us all. Of course, Mr B.V. is our Baas. His brother Mr J.V. is too young to understand this. These Indians are just like us black people and they are particular about how these things should be done. Your father could have come to me beforehand to let me know so that I would at least be ready for this. And we all have children in school, needing fees – but anyway, *m'zukuru*, the problem has been solved and you will be able to go to school and if Longman's son or my own son goes to school – it's all the same. These Indians work us very hard, you know. Very expensive school you're going to, eh?'

Mr B.V. returned with the money and counted out the crisp new ten and twenty dollar bills on the counter.

'Give him an envelope, Gideon,' Mr B.V. said.

'Thank you, Sir,' George said and Mr B.V. nodded quickly.

'So why you no say thank you to Gideon? You don't say thank you to Gideon for helping you?'

'Thank you, Sekuru Masimbi,' George said. He felt the tears welling again in his eyes but he picked up the fat white envelope, folded it and put it in his pocket.

'Be sure to take that straight to your father and tell him to come and see me first thing tomorrow,' Mr B.V. said, going back to his office.

'Give my greetings to your mother my sister,' Uncle Masimbi said. George nodded and stepped out of that dark shop into the paling light outside, away from the murmuring behind him.

***

** No man. He musn't act like this.

'So, did you eat any Indian food while you were there?' his brother said.

'Did you sit in that office with him?' said another.

'What's his office like? What does he spend the day doing?'

'Did he speak in English or did he use Indian?' his mother said.

Did you did you did you and suddenly he remembered the day his woodwork teacher at primary school had called him to his table and kept him there taunting him, saying, 'Your life is in the hands of Mr B.V... Everything you do depends on Mr B.V... That man has been paying your father peanuts for thirty years... Your clothes don't fit you... Are those second-hands Mr. B.V.'s sons shed for you?' until George had snapped back, 'It doesn't matter' and the teacher had taken his glasses off and glared at him and laughed and said, 'What? Do you dare say that to a teacher?' and had laughed again and glared at him across the table and then the teacher's face had suddenly fallen and the teacher had taken him out to the next-door classroom and said to the teacher there, 'You know what this boy said to me, you know what this boy said to me when I told him his life is in the hands of Mr B.V. ? This boy said it doesn't matter!'

And he had gone home and told his older brother about it and his brother had kept quiet until the day they fought when he broke his brother's mathematical compass and his brother had said with a bleeding nose, 'That's why you say it doesn't matter to teachers!'

Did you did you did you and he went out of the house and as he left his father was standing the bicycle against the wall, back from work and his father grinned at him and lifted two loaves of bread from the bicycle carrier, two squashed brown loaves of left-over bread some uncle who worked at a bakery had given him and his father said, 'How did your meeting with Mr B.V. go?'

'I left the envelope on the bed,' George said, and he went into the toilet, locked himself up and wept.

Among the Dead

When Mr Melbury breathed his chest whistled as if he was sucking in the air through pins. His voice squeaked when he was excited or displeased, which spoiled its otherwise rather fine English accent. But then he was an old man.

Short, a little stout, with a slight wispy crest of silver hair on his balding head, Mr Melbury had a small beaked nose and darting blue eyes which made him resemble a bird, although I could never decide what species.

I had not had many white teachers which is perhaps why I felt such ambivalence towards him. He had seen, known, many black students. I was young, strong, ambitious and, I thought, clever. I wanted to go somewhere. I wanted to be recognised. But Mr Melbury, seemed impartial, indifferent. And he was an old man, a poor specimen, not someone I thought I could look up to. If I stood near him and heard the air hissing and stabbing through his lungs and saw his back heaving, I was moved by irritation and pity. I felt somehow as if I had been let down, that if I was going to be recognised, it should be by someone whom I could respect. And in class I busied myself by coining cruel descriptions and similes. I fancied myself a writer. I was cruel because I knew Mr Melbury could see through me, and

I wanted to keep a distance. And yet, on the other hand, I wanted to break his reserve, and occasionally I even allowed myself to feel a little sorry for him.

One cold morning when I saw him walking towards the classroom, his breath steaming jerkily into the cold air, his arms laden with books, I sidled up beside him and offered to carry them for him. He turned sharply towards me, looked me up and down for a moment as if trying to ascertain how genuine my offer was, and then said crisply, 'No thank you. I always carry my own books. I can manage.'

I fell back, furious with myself. Hurt by the rejection. Unclear why in my own mind this elderly teacher should exercise so much power over me. Weren't there other teachers after all? And yet I was convinced that he too felt the ambivalence, he knew what it felt like to feel different, to be different.

I was a new student. I wanted to be a writer. I was litigious and affected by the wave of nationalism that was seeping through the land and infiltrating its every institution. I did not know what it meant to be white, to be old, to be friendless, to be cynical. Mr Melbury knew that the geography teacher at my old school had been the author of a prescribed textbook which most classes in the country were using.

I discovered that Mr Melbury and the author disagreed on certain fundamental interpretative theories and that the former's geography textbook had been rejected by the regime. I suspected that Mr Melbury saw me as an advocate for his adversary's theories.

'Come,' he would taunt, 'You were taught by a famous textbook writer. What did he have to say about the geomorphological causes of the East African Rift Valley?' Or 'What is your author's considered opinion about the existence of Gondwanaland?'

I was tongue-tied. I knew what he was referring to, but had not thought it through. It was a theory which did not seem to matter much one way or the other. This I could not say, so I muttered that I did not know, much to Mr Melbury's amusement. 'I suggest you do a little real work,' he said, 'if you want to pass your exams. Poetry will not get you very far.' There was a hint of sarcasm in his voice, and I suspected, resentfully, that he had seen some of my more puerile efforts, and wished he had not done so.

Don't get me wrong Mr Melbury was an accomplished scholar and brilliant teacher. I respected him. I wanted to impress him. I worked hard. He gave numerous assignments which he promptly marked and returned. Hating research work as I did, and preferring to spend more time on literature and writing, I chose a few weeks later to write for him an account of wine production in Southern Africa. I proceeded to assemble hastily concocted notes into solid-looking prose, broken up optimistically by maps and diagrams.

Three days later, I received the assignment back with a generous paragraph of Mr Melbury's immaculate red cursive:

A very gallant attempt to conquer the unknown. Unfortunately, chivalric excursions like this often end in catastrophe. This essay is beautifully written, marvellously full of cadence, but totally misleading. The maps and diagrams are pretty but woefully outdated. Perhaps what disturbed me most when I read your essay was my ignorance of the fact that farmers in Southern Africa could actually grow wine .. .

After reading the comment I looked and saw Mr Melbury gloating at me from across the room with a look that seemed to say, 'There, I got you now! '

***

I had then only been three weeks at the mission school, preparing for my university entrance examinations, two months away. It was in the mid-seventies. The war of liberation was intensifying. The beast of Rhodesia was sagging to its knees. Large tracts of the country were falling into guerrilla hands.

I had been tossed out of a government school, together with a hundred other sixth-formers, for staging a peaceful demonstration against moves to conscript black school-leavers into the Rhodesian army. We had marched forty miles to stage the demonstration, had been harassed by police and then unceremoniously expelled. After the expulsions some of my classmates had joined the guerrillas, others had vanished into crowded suburbs or half-known villages and a handful like me had been lucky enough to secure places at more sympathetic mission schools.

I was still bristling with anger and was naturally quick to take offence. Now don't get me wrong. Even then I knew my hostility towards Mr Melbury was somewhat irrational. After all, the mission school had accepted me. Although he himself was not in orders, he had lived and worked at the mission for nearly forty years. In that sense, he was a missionary and mission teachers were in those days regarded as liberals. But Rhodesia had taught me to see things in terms of black and white. And, like wounded prey, I was wary, suspicious, and ready to take umbrage at the slightest provocation.

I knew I had given an inadequate response to the question but the sarcastic edge to Mr Melbury's voice cut me deeply. I knew I could do better and I hated to think he took me for a fool.

I withdrew. I worked hard at my essays; he conceded them 'A' grades and seemed a little more willing to take me seriously. One Sunday after the morning service he came up behind me and said unexpectedly:

'You have such a fine bass voice, would you like to join the mission choir?'

I looked at him, surprised. His blue eyes were still but not cold. His pale lips hung open, the tongue poised – charged, I supposed – with a fresh insult. I could hear his chest sputter. I felt trapped. Should I reject the compliment, or accept it. Was he being honest?

'The choir...' I responded, 'I really don't know. I would need to think about it.'

'Ho. I see you need to think about it.' He paused. Blinked. His chest sputtered. He had made an offer. It was a gesture. It was well meant. Would I throw it back in his face?

Then he said again, 'We'd be happy to have you.'

As a young boy I had once sung in a church choir but I was not sure I wanted to join the mission choir. I was new to the school and wanted to maintain my anonymity. I took pride in not allowing myself to be swallowed up by the rituals of mission school life.

Later that week, on All Souls' Day, the school went down to the cemetery to pray for the dead. It was a bright blue morning – piety seemed to hang in the air. Like geckoes, boys and girls swarmed over the graves. Some people sat on the rocks sunning themselves, some walked idly between the rows and others leaned nonchalantly on tombstones. I was loitering among the rocks at the edge of the cemetery when Mr Melbury approached me.

'I don't think you had rituals such as these at your previous school,' he said.

'No,' I answered.

'Then you must find life here very strange.'

'Sometimes.'

He was humming softly to himself as if being in the graveyard gave him a sense of peace. He was an old man. He should not have been teaching. Perhaps he would die here. Unloved, unmourned. How many students had passed through his hands?

'There's plenty of sitting space among the graves,' he said.

I shrugged.

'You can even sit on the tombstones if you like. Or perhaps you resent having to sit among the dead? They have memories which you can never share.' He paused, 'You are superstitious?'

'Not really. I'm not afraid of the dead.'

My tone was resentful. Why couldn't he leave me alone? Didn't he know that we had an entirely different spirit world. That there was no reason to be afraid of one's ancestors. How long had he been in the country anyway? Hadn't he learnt anything?

'If you are not superstitious would you like to walk with me through the graveyard tonight... late – at midnight, when the spirits walk?' He chuckled.

'Why?' I managed a little laugh.

'Just to prove that superstitious beliefs in *varoyi* and *n'anga* are unfounded. That graveyards are receptors of bones, recipients of memories, no more.'

I shrugged. I wanted to be left alone.

The service was beginning. Mr Melbury sat down on a flat-topped boulder next to me. The crowd fell silent. The choir, conducted by a nervous, red-haired nun, broke into a melody. Early one Saturday morning I had seen the same nun going up to the geography room with Mr Melbury. He had worn a faded brown suit and from the bottom of the steps I had seen the nun's vest, like wire gauze, through her habit. Nuns and vests. Mr Melbury and the nun had talked in tones too low for my aroused, inquisitive, adolescent ears. They had smiled at each other. Always the nun wore that gauze-like vest and I wondered if she had anything else underneath. I knew that Mr Melbury sometimes ate with the nuns at the rectory. I had been to the dining room once and glimpsed the tables draped with a spotless white cloth, and laid out with gleaming cutlery and jars of water. It was somehow a cold scene – everything was spick and span. The only thing that had excited me was the bowl of crimson apples and the loaf of brown bread – though the bread had vaguely reminded me of the last supper. I had come away wondering what made people want to join orders.

The silence at the end of the hymn wrenched me back to the present, and to the prayers, the litany. Then the priest lit the incense and walking up and down the cemetery, allowed the holy scented smoke to permeate into the air. A murmur of quiet voices followed him. I liked the smell of incense and its invocation of mystery. I thought the church too is riddled by little acts of superstition. I wondered how Mr Melbury would react to this allegation.

***

He came for me at a quarter to twelve. I was in my cubicle working on an assignment when I heard his breathing. I was surprised. I thought the idea of a walk had been some kind of a joke, a challenge which I did not want to take up.

I closed my books and followed him out of the study block, away from the perimeter of light, into the night. I didn't have to slow down. He thrust himself forward resolutely, as we went past the chapel, dark and seemingly medieval, past the dormitories swaddled in sleep. In the faint light of the crescent moon his hair gleamed.

'What exactly will we do in the graveyard?' I asked.

'Prove that ghosts do not exist.'

We walked on, down the stone path, past the stagnant pond, our steps crunching on the gravel.

'Exactly twenty years ago I went for a walk like this with a student like you who is now one of your prominent nationalist politicians,' he said.

'Why?'

'It was just after the second world war. Two local Africans killed in the fighting in East Africa had been buried in this cemetery. Their deaths outside the country had sparked febrile rumours. The usual stories – of strange citings, lights in the cemetery, armed figures glimpsed among the tombstones, strange noises – and this student claimed he had observed these visitations.'

'Did anybody else claim to have seen them?'

'Yes. A local exorcist was even called in to 'quell' the spirits. And a local priest also tried to exorcise the graveyard. I walked among the dead, with the student before the exorcisms. I saw and heard nothing. Absolutely nothing.'

'So you think the claims were unfounded?' I asked.

'Of course. It was all in the imagination and that's what I told this student.'

If I had agreed with him before, if I had wanted to put myself on the side of rationality, I reacted. I felt Mr Melbury was being patronising. And that, for some reason, he saw me as a man at the crossroads. He wanted to prove that there was nothing to the African belief in *varoyi*. What did he care? What did he know?

The tombstones gleamed in the moonlight. It was a large cemetery bound by mournful *muunga* trees. Had I been in a frivolous mood I would have imagined restless spirits fleeing before the old teacher's presence. The only smell detectable was that of cold concrete, earth and weeds. Grass dappled that deadland in the moonlight and the crosses loomed over their shadows. Huge crosses towered over smaller ones. Christian crosses defended men and women from fire and brimstone. Here and there lay an old pot or a rust-eaten domestic utensil, a last hapless link with the living world. It was the small, obscure graves, shrouded in the mystery of their insignificance, which awed me.

Mr Melbury walked up the path and then sat himself down on a large bed of concrete.

'Sit down?'

'No.'

'Are you superstitious?'

'No.'

'Have you heard or noticed anything suspicious so far?'

He glanced at me quizzically.

The silence made me uncomfortable. If a bat had shrieked or a cricket shrilled it might have helped to dispel the awesome silence. Instead all I could hear was Mr Melbury's laboured breathing and the heel of his shoe tapping dryly against the concrete.

He rose and began his inspection. Every few paces he would stoop to brush leaves off a grave, trace the edge of a headstone with his finger, straighten an old pot and pause to enjoy the silence. I crunched reluctantly on the gravel behind him. I was uneasy. I didn't see him as an old rationalist with not long to live, making his peace with the world of the dead. Instead, I wondered if he was trying to impress me. Then I felt something crawl over my sandalled feet. Ants! Swarms of tiny ants. I was standing on an ant's nest! I stamped my feet. Suddenly frantic. What on earth was I doing here. I'd be exhausted tomorrow and unable to work. I would fail my exams. I felt irritable. I wanted to shout out loud, yell at the old duffer calmly pursuing some game of his own and forcing me to play it with him.

'Is anything wrong?' Mr Melbury inquired quietly.

'Just ants,' I told him, suppressing my urge to yell.

Once, when I was very young, I had visited an uncle in the country. I was given the responsibility of rounding up the calves every evening. One evening I failed to capture a reluctant, and very frisky, calf. Each time I managed to shoo it towards the entrance of the pen, it galloped away into the bushes. It grew dark.

I was eight years old and an urban child. I knew there was an old grave near the pen; one of those rare traditional structures of wood and grass placed behind the homestead, adjacent to the kraal. In my pursuit of the animal I plunged into the grave, my arms and legs tripping over the wooden framework. The old grass thatch caved in on me and my head hit the mound. I felt I was being sucked into the sand. With a yell I threw myself out of the broken grave, spitting out bits of grass, and fled home. For months I lived with the feel and smell of mouldy sand clinging to my skin.

And now, watching Mr Melbury hunched over a tombstone, like a craftsman absorbed in his work, I cursed myself for agreeing to come with him. My ears began to drum with fear. I was afraid of him.

'Mr Melbury...'

'Yes,' he answered. Did I detect triumph?

'Can we go, now? I have work to do.'

'Afraid?' Was there a sneer in his voice?

'I don't care what you'll think or say about this,' I said suddenly. I was surprised how firm my voice sounded. 'I don't see the point of this excursion. I'd like to return to the school now.'

He straightened up, surprised, stood for a moment dwarfed among the tombstones. Then he slowly walked towards me. He put his hand momentarily on my shoulder. What was in his eyes? It was hard to tell in the moonlight. Fear? Withdrawal? Acceptance? We made our way back to the school. Our feet scrunched on the gravel. I could hear his laboured breathing.

***

I sat in his library while he made tea. It was after one o'clock. The world seemed a very dark and silent place.

The walls were lined with books, hundreds of them. Most of the books were in hardback or leather casing and were arranged according to author – Austen, Conrad, Dickens, Hardy, Hugo, Lawrence, Shakespeare, and other classics. There were history and geography books, natural science books, magazines and journals. The room could have passed for a city library. I was impressed.

'Unfortunately I never lend my books to anyone,' Mr Melbury said, as he brought in the mugs of tea and eased himself into a rocking-chair.

His tone made me seethe with resentment. Of course I had no intention of borrowing his books, let alone browsing through them. I knew him well enough now.

'It took me a lifetime to build up this collection,' he continued, rocking in his chair, 'books have been my friends. Teaching can be a lonely activity.'

I shuffled in my chair. I was in no mood for nostalgia. I had never thought that whites could be lonely. In fact I had never thought about them at all, except as our oppressors. I wasn't ready to move away from the stereotypes.

'You are wondering what will happen to all these books when I die,' he continued.

The mention of death gave me a twinge of guilt or anxiety, such as all young people feel when old people talk about dying. I made an attempt to relax but he had sensed my alarm.

'As you grow older,' he said, 'death becomes a companion, almost a friend. I don't expect you to understand this now.' He paused, then went on as if he'd given away too much, as if all he'd talked about were his books. 'I shall give my books to the school library before I leave.'

Too late for me, I thought, but I said, 'Oh, are you leaving?'

'I'm returning to England this Christmas. I'm returning to a country I haven't lived in all my adult life.' He didn't say anything about loneliness, but this time I could feel it.

'But won't you stay on to see this country independent, Mr Melbury?' I heard myself saying.

He gave me a half smile. His face softened. 'That has been my wish for the past forty years. But I'm an old man now.'

I didn't believe that he could or would concede so easily to old age. I didn't consider what the future might hold once he stopped teaching. I assumed he was chickening out, like so many of his Rhodesian kindred. Liberals, or so they said, but people who now sought greener pastures. I was suddenly enraged to think that he too had fallen victim to the bigoted view that a holocaust would follow independence.

'Home is home,' he said, but I didn't quite believe him. He picked a photograph off the mantelpiece, and offered it to me. Mr Melbury looked out of the frame. He had the same twinkling eyes, beaked nose and slightly open mouth. His ears stuck out sadly from under a thatch of fair hair. I guessed he was thirty or so when the picture was taken, but already I saw a shadow of despair darkening his face.

'That was the year I joined this school,' he explained, his voice filling the silence.

I finished my tea. I knew he wanted us to talk. There were the books. There was his life. There was the history of the school. There was me... but I told him I had to go.

'Very well.'

'Thanks for the walk, anyway,' I grinned.

'You can always pop in for a cup of tea and a chat. In these last few weeks...' his voice tailed away.

He opened the door and saw me out. He watched me clatter down the stone path towards the grove. When I turned he was still standing in the doorway of his sprawling house, his figure silhouetted in the dim light. I wondered what he would do. Make himself another pot of tea? Read a book? Rock in his chair? Go to bed?

My head was full of unanswered questions about his life. I was assailed by doubts and misgivings about my behaviour towards him. I was confused. Flattered to have been singled out. Annoyed to think l might have been manipulated. Ashamed at my abruptness. I felt that he doled out his gestures of friendliness very carefully. It did not occur to me that lonely people are often eccentric, they lose the graces of society, not that I had shown very many. And I was self-confident enough to think that there could be an understanding between a young man of seventeen, and an old man of seventy: but wasn't that what he was reaching for as well?

I opened the door of the dormitory and slid thankfully into my bed. The other boys were asleep, its smell hit me in the face. The snoring from the beds, arranged symetrically like graves, was grotesque. It was two in the morning and the night hung stiff at the windows. Maybe I would go and have a cup of tea with him before the end of the term, before he left the country.

***

Five years later, two years after independence had been achieved with relative ease: after twenty-four months of painstaking integration and

the voluntary leakage of the faithless, I met Mr Melbury in the capital.
He was standing on a pavement in First Street, watching men and
machines at work on a construction site. His back was turned to me.
The hunch of the shoulders caught my attention. He turned and his
blue eyes, behind thick lenses, fell on me. Clutching my briefcase in
both hands, I stopped.

'I know you,' he said, stiffly, uncomfortably. Every teacher is always so much more known than their pupils. He looked me up and
down in an effort to remember. There was a trace of amusement in
his eyes. I must have looked a little earnest in my suit, though I was
taller and bearded now.

'Don't tell me who you are. Let me remember your name.' He was
trying.

I gave him ten more seconds, then giving history a self-conscious
poke I said, 'Mr Melbury, I presume...'

'Why, I even recognise your voice,' he exclaimed, 'You were at the
mission school. Wasn't it you I .... Oh yes. I remember!'

'Have you forgotten Gondwanaland, or wine-growing farmers, our
midnight walk in the graveyard?'

A light washed over his face and he laughed.

He told me he had just arrived from England, for a short visit.
He now lived in London. He had come to see how things were in
Zimbabwe. He asked me about myself. He was surprised to hear that
I had already finished university and had worked for a year, among
other things teaching and writing.

'Written a book!' he gasped, and I told him it was on the shelves. I
told him by the time I came to the mission school I was already well
into the first draft. I couldn't overcome the urge to boast; to show
him that I was now a somebody. But he said he wanted to read my
book and that there was a friend of his called Mrs Holden who ran
a bookshop four blocks away and if I went there and autographed a
copy she could pay for it and mail it to him.

And so I left him gazing at the construction site, and rushed to
fulfill a string of commitments. A man at peace with his condition,
I thought while I with my ludicrous briefcase, was burning my soul

up in the name of success.

***

Six weeks later, I received a letter from Mr Melbury, through Mrs Holden. He had read my book, he said, and liked it.

'It is so vividly fresh and honest, I wonder what your next work will be like...' I pondered the compliment, remembering the paranoia of waiting for reviews that never came, of dreading the sight of my own book lying stale and sunbleached in the window of some dingy shop, of spying on scarcely dwindling stock, of masquerading as a librarian and tricking shop attendants into making orders ...

'It reminded me of my early days at the mission school when I used to go out with a young student, a friend of mine to his home in the countryside. The rhythms of the seasons and of work which you describe took me back years. The *ambuya* you describe reminded of my friend's grandmother...' I closed my eyes and saw Mr Melbury strutting in the sunshine of a savanna scene, a self-made anthropologist, wondered at, pitied and loved.

I heard my own words. Who was patronising who? The Englishman who always 'struts' into the 'savanna scene', who is always out of place, no matter how hard he tries. I was trying to write a radio script, at the time, and I realised that I was thinking in clichés. Perhaps I had always done so. Had Mr Melbury tried to challenge me to think differently? I felt a tremor of uncertainty. But a young white man feeling at home in the rural areas, a young white man who took a black man seriously enough to go home with him... well, that was a dimension to his character that I had missed altogether.

'I'm surprised you never told me you were writing. I did think there was something distinctive in your prose style, even in your geography essays. You have chosen an absorbing career but you will need to be humble and patient if you intend to live from your writing...'

What would he know? And what would he know of the tangle of my commitments, my fantasies about cars and women which contradicted and undermined the values portrayed in that first book? What would Mr Melbury say, if he knew? I was disturbed that this man, whom I had not thought about for five years, who taught me for one term, could affect me so much. Why should I care what he thought? It was an unpolitically correct, childish dependence, and the same old resentment that I had once felt wormed its way into my consciousness.

He went on to comment on the political scene, and to advise that 'the world is watching you...' Irritably I put the letter down. We did not need to be told what do to. I remembered him saying 'Home is home' and I was still not convinced that this was reason enough for him to leave a place he had known for four decades.

***

Several weeks later, I sat down to write to him. Had he not asked me to? I looked for his letter, I looked everywhere but could not find it. I went to see Mrs Holden, whom I knew had the address, but was told she was on leave and would be back in three weeks. I waited for her return.

Three weeks later, Mrs Holden looked at me over her cash register, her grey locks tucked behind her ears. Her eye-lids fluttered when I told her the purpose of my visit.

'You want Mr Melbury's address,' she said, in a hushed voice, 'Oh dear, I must tell you about Mr Melbury....'

***

I rummaged through my chest of drawers, unearthing sheaves of mail, ordinary and threatening, from estate agents and the power supply company, old Christmas cards, loose receipts, unfiled certificates and dog-eared photographs. I shook out large bulging envelopes full of strange bits of bureaucracy – copies of my lease to life – birth certificates, blood-group cards, insurance policies, testimonials, university contracts, disused lenses, condoms sweating through khaki wrappers, notebooks filled with half-forgotten addresses, old letters, broken necklaces, stubs of friendship...

I wrenched open the headboard of my bed and dredged it of old magazines, poems brittle as dead leaves, shoe-brushes, lost identity cards, pornographic clippings, publishers' rejection slips among twists of underwear...

Then I thought it might be in my suitcase, so I pulled out the suitcase and tipped the contents onto the bed. But there was little there besides the smell of old new clothes rashly bought and hastily abandoned. I combed the wardrobe, turning out pockets, trying to remember what I had worn the day I ...

Then I thought yes, it might be on my reading desk and I swept through a new morass of paper, pricking my fingers on loose staples and staining them with carbon paper ... I felt a surge of guilt and anger – a hard lump in my throat which I could not cough up or swallow. My eyes were dry, I knew I would not weep. I looked at the mess on the bed, at the excavation around me, the litter of my life, and despaired. I felt that if I found it, I might stumble upon the key to our failed friendship.

I tried to remember what I had been writing then and delved into my last manuscripts, pages of scrawl in a tattered blue file and there, between two stinging newspaper reviews of my first work, were the crisp blue sheaves of Mr Melbury's unanswered letter.

Brothers and Sisters

Zacheus was only twenty-two or twenty-three, barely a man, when he saw the light.

It flashed from the sky, knocked him to his knees, wrestled with his soul, wrenched the worm of darkness therein, dazzled and blinded him.

When he regained his sight, after no more than a few hours, Zacheus was a new man – Brother Zacheus. A flame lit his soul and radiated its glow through his head and limbs and a new-found purity flowed through his veins. His fingers felt soft and light, his step graceful, as he walked proudly along the dirty littered streets, past the muttering vulgarity of the graffiti scrawled on the walls.

His voice mellowed, as if a sweet oil had been poured down his throat. His lips curled beautifully and shaped every syllable they emitted. When he sang, his soul swelled, and the ardour of his song made the air around him quiver.

At school, before he'd seen the light, Zacheus had learnt to play the guitar. But now a new tenderness settled on his fingers and he would sit on the rocks, strumming up to heaven.

His small room was clean, though frugally furnished with a narrow bed, a sagging bookshelf, a folding table and matching stool, a chest of drawers and two easy chairs. Not without a tinge of regret had he taken down his prized poster of Che Guevara that had always given him a revolutionary tingle, and hung up one of Christ distributing the loaves and fishes, freely available, and in full colour, from his church.

Zacheus had been working as a lab technician for two years, long enough to establish friendships with his workmates, before he saw the light. And once he came to accept that they willingly chose another less enlightened path, a kind of truce existed between them. But when he looked through the microscope, he no longer saw micro-organisms but the grand scheme of things, a revelation of the order of the world.

It was this that made him aware that something was missing in his life. He began to feel that perhaps he had not been born for the laboratory, that he should have been a missionary or a clergyman, and he dreamed of sainthood or martyrdom.

But his hour of revelation was not far away. And one day he felt a final swelling of his soul, a quivering in his vocal chords and his tongue leapt up to the roof of his mouth charged with the Word, he heard a voice calling from within him for souls. Souls, souls, souls! Human souls to be brought back to the light. Erring souls to be won over and saved. Straying souls to be brought back to the righteous path.

So Brother Zacheus resigned from his job, and took up part-time employment to give him more time to hunt in earnest for souls.

He waylaid his former workmates and pleaded with them to regard the safety of their souls. He wept for them when they merely glanced at his pamphlets. He prayed for their souls. He prayed that they might be struck down on their knees and wrestled with until the stubborn worm of darkness was removed from their souls.

Meeting a wall of wicked resistance, he broadened his hunt. He sought out people in their offices, on the streets, in their homes, and he impressed upon them the desperate state of their lives. Some he found in their flats drinking, some on their way to hotels and night clubs, others wallowing lethargically on their sofas with eyes glued to their TV sets. Bravely he would mount stairs, enter alleys and risk guard dogs, confounding his hosts with the timeliness of his visits.

***

'And what might your name be, sister?' he inquired, planting himself next to a girl in the library of a small private college where he taught one or two classes in the evening.

'Sabina.' The girl's eyes lit up at the sight of the soft-spoken, carefully dressed young lecturer.

'You are not in my O-Level Maths class, are you, Sister Sabina?' he asked with a wide ingenuous smile.

She shook her head.

Placing the small, regular pile of pamphlets on the table in front of him, he straightened them with gratuitous ease. Then he opened one of them and murmured piously, under his breath.

Sabina struggled to concentrate on her books. Fascinated by his soft fingers and awed by his proximity, she shifted her legs under the table. His genteel manner ruffled her eighteen-year-old heart and made it quiver with expectation. Her eyes danced around him, sweeping across his pamphlets, and away.

And what might you be reading, Sister Sabina?' he softly interrupted her again, while observing the thick sacred silence of the library. Reaching over to her he slowly drew a thin paperback from the middle of her small pile. It was a popular romance with the picture of an impassioned raven-haired woman on the cover.

'Is it a good story, Sister Sabina?'

She pursed her lips uncertainly and shrugged.

'You might enjoy reading this instead, Sister Sabina,' he said, thrusting two of his pamphlets in front of her. 'I hope you've heard of our fellowship. We are interested in saving souls, bringing people into the light' and then, after a pause, 'I would like you to come to one of our meetings.'

She looked dutifully at the pamphlets. Then, deciding perhaps that her chemical equations would deliver her from her uncertainty, she began a renewed attack on the one that had almost spoiled her day. A heavy silence fell between them as they heard each other breathing.

'I see you're having a problem with your chemistry, Sister Sabina,' he said, providently. 'Have faith and we'll solve it.'

He gently pulled the book away from her, and examined the equation. Realising that he could make little more headway in the still silent library, he offered to give her extra help. So it was that he learnt that she lived in the avenues, not far from his flat and an arrangement was made.

***

The following Monday, he made his way to the flat where Sabina lived with her older sister. He found her alone, just settling down to her files.

'How are you this evening, Sister Sabina?' he inquired, planting himself on the sofa.

'Fine, and you?'

Sabina did not know what to call this young teacher. The word 'Brother' stuck in her throat just as 'Sister' jarred in her ears. She regarded him with a mixture of curiosity and unease, flattered but made uncomfortable by his assiduous attentions.

'I see you're already doing your chemistry homework, Sister Sabina,' he said.

'I'm writing my exams in a few weeks.'

'You need not fear failure, Sister. Have faith and you will pass. And, if there's something you don't understand, I'm here to guide you. Seek and ye shall find, knock and doors will be opened unto you.'

He was good at chemistry, and he enjoyed explaining precipitates and formulae, and she was an eager pupil.

Later when she opened the fridge to get him a cream soda, he saw two wine bottles on the lower rack, among the other drinks. Another reason for returning, he thought to himself.

'Can you come again and teach me about titration?' She asked as she observed him relaxing on the sofa.

'Of course,' Brother Zacheus nodded. He had learnt that you could not rush these things and that it would be a grave mistake to introduce a solemn or religious subject too quickly. Already, she was standing dismissively in the middle of the room.

He knew he had to go. Knowing that he would pray for her later that night, he did not despair, but left in cheerful spirits, wishing her a good night's sleep and a fruitful day at the college.

He visited her twice more. But each time he ran into a wall. Whenever he cleared his throat and reached for the pamphlets in his pocket she stalled him with a diversion.

He began to think that the devil was lurking in her books and files, and that he must clear the route to her heart by concluding the mortal business of study first.

When he arrived at her flat for the fourth time, determined to convert her at all costs, he was met at the door by the loud sound of a stereo, and three or four male voices. Hesistantly, he knocked on the door. Sabina appeared in front of him in the sharp red light flooding from the room. She was wearing a white T-shirt, bright red shorts and had nothing on her feet. He gazed at her for a moment, nervously fingering the buttons of his suit.

'Oh, it's you, Zachy,' she laughed, an unusual glow in her normally quiet eyes. She had done something to her face and there was a touch of wine on her breath.

'I thought you might have time for a serious chat with me, Sister Sabina,' he told her. The male voices coming from the room hurt him. And he was touched by an unexpected sense of loss.

'You must come in and join us, Zachy.'

'You seem to have visitors.'

'Just friends of mine and my sister's.'

'Another day, then,' said Brother Zacheus quickly, and he turned and hurried down the steps, out onto the street, towards the peace of his own flat.

He would have to pray even harder for her.

He did not see her again, however. When he returned a week later a man told him that the two girls had moved to another block in the avenues.

Perhaps, thought Brother Zacheus as he crept home, Sabina's time had not come yet. Perhaps, he thought as he crept home slowly with a wounded heart, perhaps she had not been placed in his scheme of work...

So he waited. He knew that sooner or later he would have to look around him a little. After all, even the birds of the air did not have food placed in their nests for them!

***

There were several sisters in the fellowship, and perhaps a dozen who were not married, and as the conversions gained momentum, they were joined by others. Brother Zacheus regarded all the women as sisters. Every night when they met, singing or testifying to each other, praying or merely sitting in silent worship, or just having cake and tea, his relationship with each of them was one of amicable respect.

But as one by one, the future of the sisters was spiritually revealed to them and they paired off with the brothers, Brother Zacheus began to feel the first itchings of need. And he began to view the sisters in the fellowship with more discerning eyes.

That summer the fellowship had a big boost. Assisted by a range of interesting expeditions, many saw the light and joined its ranks. On one fellowship outing Brother Zácheus sat next to one of the more recent converts, Sister Monica. He plucked his guitar and they hummed a solemn tune, as the bus hurtled down towards the camp in the valley.

Sister Monica was roughly his age, perhaps a year or two older. When the light had struck her, she had been on the very edge of destruction. Her life had been riddled with problems. She had confessed as much to the fellowship. Had it not been for the street crusade which had saved her, she would have drowned in sin. Now she looked on her past with the gratitude of the saved. The fellowship had welcomed her, buried her past, and given her a clean slate on which to begin again.

Brother Zacheus listened to her sing.

She sang so sweetly, her hands humbly folded in her lap, her face radiant with peace, he felt she was good.

He heard her talk, with her slow, sweet voice and he felt she was good. And he breathed in the pure, clean scent of her body, and he *knew* she was good.

At the end of the camp meeting, he left with a new revelation; that in fact, Sister Monica was his chosen partner! Yes, they had been guided to the camp to discover their mutual destiny!

Confident of the revelation, he began to appreciate her fine womanhood. She was pure and lean, ethereal in her white dress, and with her hair done and her eyes flashing, she had the candour of a virgin angel.

In her presence, he felt he was face to face with woman as she was meant to be – clean in body and soul and thought and deed. He could recover his manhood. It made him feel proud to have waited so long and so patiently for the right woman to be revealed to him. He would offer her his clean body and a lifetime's chastity. He felt as pure as a newborn baby.

Their love grew by leaps and bounds. She visited him in his room and shared the evenings with him. She made him good meals, and brought him delicacies from her own kitchen. She tidied up and helped him do his shopping.

But never once in those incredibly warm weeks did they do more than touch hands. Schooled in the art of patience, he knew there was time for physicalities. Abstinence was even easier for Sister Monica. Every evening they would sit on the same sofa, side by side, without touching each other. When it was time to go to bed, they would accompany each other, from his room to hers and hers to his, delaying the moment of parting as great lovers do before a great separation.

When Brother Zacheus brought his clothes over for washing and ironing, at Sister Monica's request, he began to truly appreciate the pleasures of matrimony. How much more time he would have for worship, relieved rightfully of the feminine duties of washing and cooking!

The brothers and sisters in the fellowship saw the affair grow and prayed earnestly for the couple.

At last, when Sister Monica was wondering if he would ever do so, Brother Zacheus proposed.

'Will you marry me, Monica?'

She stepped forward and put her head on the firm wall of his chest. She looked up expectantly. 'Will you marry me Zachy?'

'Yes,' he smiled, his strong heart throbbing desirously against her ears.

'Lost and sinful as I used to be, Zacheus?'

'Why, all of us were lost once, Monica, before we saw the light.'

'Will you forgive my past, Zacheus?'

'That has already been forgiven, Monica. What need you fear?'

She put her arms around him, bringing the full, soft weight of her body against his and he knew days and nights of boundless bliss awaited him.

But not yet. Not before she became rightfully his at the altar, in front of the other fellows. Only then could he take her. He took one step back, held her by the shoulders and asked, as if to bring the day closer, 'Will you marry me at the end of this month, Monica, my revealed one?'

He extracted from his pocket a glittering ring, took up her hand and planted it firmly on her finger.

'Oh Zacheus.'

'Will you marry me at the end of the month, Monica mine?'

'Oh Zacheus.'

'Tell me you will, Monica dear. Tell me you will.'

'Oh Zacheus.'

'Why, Monica? Oh why, my revealed one?'

'I could marry you but I can't, Zachy.'

'Your sins were washed in the blood of the lamb. Why then must you worry? Let bygones be bygones.'

'My wretchedness is too great for forgiveness.'

'No sins can be too great to be forgiven. You know that, Monica.'

'You will never look at me again once you know the miserable creature I am. Oh, Zacheus, forgive me.'

'But you've seen the light, haven't you?'

'Yes, but...?'

'What is it, Monica?'

'I'm too vile for words, Zachy.'

'Tell me. I command you, Monica. What is it?'

There was a long silence. Confident in his manhood, Zacheus waited patiently. No sin was too great for his broad shoulders.

'I have a baby, Zacheus. Before I joined the fellowship, I had a baby. She's two years old and living with my mother. I had hoped to tell you about her but I left it too late. Now you know the truth, Zacheus.'

'A baby...,' he uttered slowly, his lips shaping every syllable.

He leapt away from her and groped for the door. He ran down the steps into the roaring night. Blindly he tore across the road. Cars screamed around him, swerving, lurching, and veering away from the figure running unheeded down the tarmac. Flashing beams searched his body with their stark white light. He heard voices shouting at him, the crash of distant laughter, and the sharp smell of hot rubber stung his nostrils. He turned off into a dark lane.

He was not sure how long he ran. His pace slowed but he continued as if he would never tire. He wanted to leave the city behind him. He wanted to get away. Following a path, he came to a thickly wooded clearing. He lost one shoe and then the other, but he ran on. The wood-strewn ground cracked and popped under his feet and drooping branches tore open his shirt, and clawed at his exposed skin. The fierce sweet smell of a pine tree maddened him. He sank at last to the ground, moaning, and pounded at the yielding earth with his fists.

He saw the pines looming over him, laughing darkly. Twinkling stars splashed over the immense sky reminded him of eternity and the littleness of his life. He stiffened with shame at his retreat.

'You will hate me forever. You will wish I had never been revealed to you, Zach.' Shutting his eyes tightly, he tried to pray. A rising anger clamped his mouth shut.

He staggered back to his feet, damp, soiled and sapped, like some night animal burrowing out of the darkness.

He did not want to see her again. Never ever. Never again would he have anything to do with Woman.

But his fury raged beyond her, beyond his own humiliation, beyond the trees and mocking stars.

Baffled by the mystery of his anger, his soul quaked. As he plodded back into the threatening maze of city lights, his sticky hands closed slowly, knotting into fists.

Snow

Corn.

Corn, corn, corn.

Square fields of corn stretching to the rims of the earth. Flat as a board.

Rocking little plane. Limousine. Campus hotel. Temporary lodge.

'Hi. How yer doin'? I'm your room mate Mark. Wanna beer?'

Mark on the phone. Wanting money from mom. Shit this. Shit that. Shit, shit. Shit here. Shit there. Clothes all over the floor. Cans. Underwear. Walkman. Yelling at the T.V. Flickering at channels. Shitshitshit.

Heat.

Ninety degrees Farenheit. Humid heat. Like walking through a curtain of hot air. No sweat. Hotter than Chiredzi or Zambezi.

'So, how hot does it get in Africa?'

Mayflower. Mostly graduate students. Sophomores. Many foreigners. Christoph Fohr. German grad. Geography and something. Small moustache. Hitler's grandson? Soft-spoken but English very bad. Simple. Quietly cynical. Smoulderingly anti-American. Same pair of shorts the whole week. Favourite hobby – sleeping and relaxing. Ephraim Mehta. Indian. Earnest red eyes. Incurable toothache.

Taught science in Nigeria. Now studying computer science.

The heat. Does it ever get cold here?

Heat. Shorts everywhere. Shorts, shorts, shorts.

Legs.

White flesh white flesh white flesh. Blue eyes. Green eyes. Black eyes. Brown. Blonde hair. Brunette. Red. Black. Multivitamin smiles. Braced teeth. Sun-tan.

Food.

Foodfood foodfood foodfood.

French-fries, fritters, frankfurters, fish, fillet, farina, falafels, figs, fennel, flax, fanta, fruitbread.

Fat.

Fat fat fat.

Fudge-face, milk-nose, coke-lips, burger-bums, popcorn-belly, choc-cheeks, gum-teeth, cream-tongue, pizza-palate, budweiser-chin, candy-kiss.

Two per cent fat free. 100% natural. Cholestrol-free calories. 99% germ free.

White flesh white face white smile.

Black face. Black-face white smile.

Hi. How yer doing? Pretty good. Nice talking to you. See yer later.

Green. Green-green-green. Green heat. Aching green summer. Daylight dragging long and lazy over the green river banks. Days fat as ducks waddling on cobblestone walkways, gobbling up seed and bread from white hands. Green summer aching like the couple waiting for dusk. Green scent aching in the air.

So, where's the snow?

African Association. Andrew. Albert. Amoke.

Agendas. Anybody from Algeria?

Africa must be free. Action now. Abolish apartheid. Artists against Apathy.

South Africans. Accomplished exiles. Thami from Jo'burg. Articulate gangster, born survivalist. USAID scholarship. Former car smuggler and racketeer. Cripple the system. Steal cars. Thami of Bolshevik trench coats and red-starred berets. Thami of the discotheque meat-markets, slaughtering blue-eyed beauties with his pocketed fists. Fuck America too. Thami, sly butcher of erotic white socialites. The mince of production. Thami in jail for slapping a white girlfriend in the face. Charged for sexual harrassment. Invasion of private space. Infringement of individual constitutional rights. Fines. Lawyers. Thami, agenda of an impromptu African Association meeting. Any contributions send to Andrew. Our father who art in USAID...

South Africans.

Abdul. Passionate Indian now turned black. Articulate marxist. Dark-eyed hauntings of the physics and anatomy of his own late adolescence. Yvonne. Slim madam of the boutiques. Doctor boyfriend at home. No politics, please. Please no politics. Politics please no.

Smanga. Patience. Ruth. Housewives. Mermaids in Levi shorts, flashing their strong dark lurid fins among white shoals. Driven to the edge with longing. Eyes heavy and bright with want. Living for the next telephone call. Head-size photos of handsome husbands on headboards. Wedding rings. Dancing in a barbed-wire fence of wedding rings at parties. We're married, please. Please we're married.

African Association parties. Rhumba. Soca. Reggae. Franco, Kuti, Bel, Mapfumo, Dibango, Masekela, Makeba. Mama Africa. Jah. The coal train coming. Africa as one. Another keg of draft, please. Pass the hat around. This is African, brother, but this ain't Africa. Dig into your pockets. Dig the vibe?

Foreign students. Ganging up. African, German, French, Caribbean, Chinese, Filipino. Etc. etc. etc. Levelled by language. United by common hatred of America. Loving, hating, the USA. Love-hating, hate-loving America. America, one big hamburger. America one big porno movie. America one big hypocrite. America one big bully. America one big racist. America one big contradiction. America this, America that.

Marko, quiet Colombian engineer with computer-brained memory: 'So, how many bridges in Africa?'

'So, what is the colour of the soil in Africa?'

'So, do Africans eat tomato sauce?'

Snow

'What is the capital city of Africa?'

'What tribe do you belong to?'

Oh, Africa. Africa of hunger, and coups and wars. Ignorance and disease. Oh, Africa, when will you learn?

***

Snow.

Snow at last.

Snow falling. Piling up. Covering everything. White snow. As white as snow. Red as a rose, white as snow. Cold as snow. Snow jackets. Layers. Gloves. People fat as astronauts. Jacket on, jacket off, jacket on. Frozen ears. Frozen air hitting lungs. Careful. Whipped red faces. Red as whipped faces. Shuttered rooms. Trapped air. Radiators. Thermostats. Beautiful, if you can stay warm. Beautiful, if you can pay central. Must be poor people freezing out there. Death, even. Harlem. Frost at Mbare.

Snow. Cold, loneliness. No legs, no laughter. Layers of loneliness packing into cakes of ice. The hard ice of longing. Cold and hard as pornography. Magazines splattered with blood-red flesh. Peep shows. Live.

Can the earth be so dead, so cruel? So white? Were shorts possible? Oh, for a black face, for laughter, for warmth.

The Waterfall

He seemed at first to be just one of those obnoxious attention-seekers
one meets at a braai – the ones who know all the jokes and anecdotes
doing the rounds. They can wisecrack about footballers, presidents,
vice-presidents, ex-presidents, ailing couples, migratory workers,
dealers and what not; they know about whose baby isn't whose, who
stole how much, who killed who and, of course, who bribed who.
They will cadge drinks, eye other men's partners and burn their fingers on other people's pork. This one was twenty-five or twenty-sev-
en, short and slim and rather likable for his audacity and his complete
disregard of himself, though he did have a cell phone hitched onto
his jeans.

I was meandering round the braai area, sipping a warming beer,
untempted by the smell of roasting meat, alone, undecided and jaded. I was still sober, but already afraid to go home; I was unsure
whether to go in and listen to the clanking band and risk another
late night, or to buy some take-aways and drive on to some other
spot. I wondered if I should go home. There was a small crowd
round the fire, listening to the young man and I thought, hearing
snatches of his delivery, but isn't he afraid of the CIO, the gentlemen in suits? He was beginning to tell another story, everyone was

rapt and I thought, why not, and moved closer.

***

Once I was in Nyanga, attending a sales rep course. They put us up at the casino hotel. There were mostly old people on the course – people about to kick the bucket. The sessions were long and boring. You know how tedious such courses are – telling us what we already know and wasting our time and their money instead of raising our commission.

I was fed up with hotel food, so one evening I decided to go to the township to eat sadza and *mazondo*. I jumped into my 626; it was a brand new metallic blue one, automatic executive. I hit the juice. Driving through the park, I startled three duiker feeding near a clump of rocks near the road. Within fifteen minutes I was in the township. There was a bar and young men and women going in and out. You know these small town bars – girls were looking at my 626 and I was cool for a while, judging the scene. Then I saw two chicks that I liked and I called one of them over and said, '*Hes* baby,' and she said, '*Muribho here blaz?*' and I said, '*Ko ndeipi?*' and she said, '*Hapana mufunge.*' and I said, 'Don't worry. *Tinozvigadzirisa.*'* She had a nice round face and short hair and a sucker in her teeth and was wearing a white T-shirt, a black palazo and matching black tackies. I said to her, 'So what's your name, baby?' and she said, 'Martha.' I opened the left door and said, 'Jump in.' She said, 'Can I get my friend?' and I said, 'Which one?' and she pointed her out and said, 'We always move together,' and I said, 'All right.' She called her friend and the friend came over and said her name was Saru, short for Sarudzai. Saru also had short hair, and was light-skinned and rather sad-looking, but smiled when I talked to her. I said to them, 'So where's the move tonight?' and they said, 'There's a disco at Chako's Place,' and I said, 'Where's that?' and they said, 'We'll show you.' So I hit the juice again and we went about five k's towards the mountains and I said, 'Is that the famous Nyangani Mountain?' and they laughed and Martha said, 'No, the Nyangani Mountain reaches right up to the sky,' and Martha

---

* 'Hi baby' and she said 'Are you OK, blaz?' and I said 'So what's up?' and she said, 'Nothing' and I said, 'Don't worry. We'll see about that.'

said, 'What've you heard?' and I said, 'Well, people disappearing and strange animals seen...' and Saru cut me and said, smiling, in her sad sort of way, 'Don't talk about it.'

We got to the disco and parked outside and went in to buy sadza and *mazondo*. They were real cheap so we bought a plateful of them and ate together sitting at one of the tables. Then we bought some beers and started dancing in the corner. The beer was cheap too and the place started filling up and we were talking and laughing together and Martha and Saru kept close to me. We were getting high and Martha was talking a lot, but Saru was quiet, steadily drinking her beers as they came. I knew then that they were experienced drinkers and that I would have to go with the two of them.

You know how time flies when you are enjoying yourself at a disco. Before I knew it, it was closing time. It must've been between two and three in the morning. I had some empties in the car, so I got them and Martha negotiated some take-aways from the barman. We sat in the car drinking the take-aways and listening to rumba.

'Let's go and get a puff,' said Martha.

We drove slowly back to the township. There was a jumble of medium-size houses, four-roomed houses, mud and grass thatch rondavels.

'Give me twenty dollars,' said Martha. I pulled out a wad. 'Wait here,' she said.

She slipped out into the dark. I switched off the headlights; it was pitch dark outside. A wooden door opened and shut. A cock crowed. She was gone a good ten minutes. I closed my hand over Saru's and said, 'Is she coming back?'

'She will,' said Saru. 'What's taking her so long?', I asked.

Saru put her two hands over one of mine and squeezed it gently.

I said, 'Is this where you live?' and she shook her head. I said, 'How long have you known Martha?' She said, 'Since we were little.' I said, 'So, you live with your mother and father?' and she nodded. I said, 'So what will they say?' and she smiled. Then Martha appeared from behind the car. She came to my side and mistakenly struggled with my door, then went round to hers.

'Switch on the light,' she said. I put on the headlights and she said, 'No. Inside the car.' I switched on the light inside the car and she made the joint.

'Mai Norah thought you might be a cop,' she said. Are you a cop?' I shook my head. Saru said, 'Even cops smoke.' Martha ruffled my hair and said, 'Was Saru nice to you while I was away?' I laughed. And she said again, `Saru, were you nice to our man while I was away?'

She lit up. She took three or four pulls and handed it to Saru, who did the same and handed the weed back to me. Now I'm not an *mbanje* person. I've taken it several times when I'm with somebody who likes it, but I don't go hunting for it. I don't like mixing it with alcohol either. And I was already high on eight or ten pints. But I said, why not, and pulled at the stub. It hit me instantly.

'It's Malawi gold,' said Saru, nodding slowly. She reached over from the back seat and put her hands round my shoulders. Martha rummaged through the cassettes in my glove cabin and put on an Afro jazz album.

'Hugh Masekela,' Saru said, slowly.

'You like him?' I asked, my head reeling.

'You think because we live in a high-density area in a small town we don't understand music?' said Martha.

'Can I lie down for ten minutes?' I asked. The east was turning purple. I knew I would need some rest before attempting to start back to the hotel.

Martha reached over my waist and lowered my back seat. I pulled her down and buried her face in my stomach, then turned round to wrap an arm round Sarudzai, in the back seat.

When I woke up it was nine o'clock, and the sun was flooding into the car. A few people were walking outside in the dust road. I was surprised to see how dilapidated some of the houses were. Martha was sitting up, changing cassettes. Saru was curled up on the back seat, snoring gently. I had a splitting headache.

'Get up Saru,' said Martha, turning round to shake her friend. Saru woke up and yawned. In the morning, she looked about seventeen but she looked tired. Martha looked like she hadn't slept a wink. She was about eighteen. I could tell the good times were taking a toll on the girls. Saru had scars on her hands.

'Are you going to work?' Martha asked me.

'Later,' I said, recklessly, hoping I could miss the first few sessions of the seminar without anybody noticing.

'Let's find something to eat,' said Martha. I gave her some money and she brought back three Fantas, six doughnuts and a bar of bathing soap. We wolfed down the food. I felt better.

'Let's go and have a bath,' said Martha.

'Where?' I asked.

'There's a waterfall not far away from here,' said Martha.

'You'll like it,' said Saru.

'Is it safe?' I asked.

'We grew up here. We go there every now and then. Remember the last time we went there, Saru?'

Saru nodded absent-mindedly.

We drove back to the tarred road, as if going back towards the hotel for about three kilometres, then branched off onto a dirt track. Then we parked the car near a cliff and slid and slipped our way down a bushy slope to the river. I could hear the water thundering over the rocks and as we pushed through the undergrowth, there it was – a gigantic python of water swinging round shining black granite boulders, crashing towards us and then tumbling away into the undergrowth.

Martha slipped out of her clothes, stepped knee deep into the water and started soaping herself. Saru followed slowly. I sat on a boulder, watching them, one dark fish and one light-skinned one, the water glittering on their nubile bodies.

'So what are you doing sitting there?' grinned Martha, spraying water at me with her fingers. 'Take off your clothes!'

I took off my shirt, then slowly kicked off my trousers and shoes and stepped into the water.

Martha vigorously soaped my chest and my back, then did Saru's. I took the soap from her, scrubbed them both and poured water over their heads. I felt them gasp and shudder and laugh as the water coursed over their strong young breasts. When we were clean we sat on the rock washing our clothes. Suddenly, I noticed drops of blood on the rock not far from where we sat, large drops of dried blood dissolving into the water, bloodied chicken feathers, and the remnants of a dead fire. My heart skipped a beat. I saw the blood and the feathers but I continued to wash Saru's skirt, and Martha's palazo and gave no sign of what I'd seen. I slipped over the rock, away from the blood, towards Saru. It must have been while I was moving that Martha made her own, invisible move.

The next moment there was Martha towering behind us, naked, gleaming wet and spread-eagled, brandishing a green stick. She cut Saru quickly on the back, thrice, then hit me in the crotch. I leapt up to grab her but she cut me on the breast and on the hands. She was breathing like a train and her eyes were wide open like marbles. When I grabbed her hands there was so much power in them I had a hard time subduing her. I twisted her arms and she let go of the stick.

'Why are you beating us?' I gasped. 'Why are you beating Saru? Why are you beating me?'

She did not answer, but instead went limp in my arms. I let her free and she fell to her knees, swaying. I said to Saru, 'Why is Martha doing this?'

Saru did not answer, but only fingered her bruises. Then she said, 'Oh, my shoes.'

The water had swept her tackies off to the middle of the waterfall. One of them was caught between the forked branch of a bush. The other was bobbing among the reeds like a little boat. If we did not do something soon the shoes would be lost.

'Wait,' said Martha. '*Ndichadzitora.*'†

She picked up the stick and plunged into the water, after the shoes. I said, 'Be careful!' But she seemed to know what she was doing. She reached over and fished the first shoe out of the reeds and threw it onto the bank. She tried to reach out for the second one, but could not disentangle it from the bushes. She said to Saru, 'Come and hold

---

† I'll fetch them.

me.' Saru stepped cautiously into the water, put one foot out and gripped Martha's waist. I said again, 'Be careful.' Saru sniffed and squeezed tears out of her eyes. Martha turned to her and touched her on the shoulder and said, 'I'm sorry, Saru, *sha*. Don't cry.'

Martha fished and fished for the shoe but could not disentangle it. She seemed to get more angry and impatient with each futile thrust. I considered stepping in to help but hesitated, not sure how she would react. She reached out for a deeper foothold and yelled at Saru, 'I said hold me!'

'Leave it,' I said. 'Let the shoe go.'

'I said hold me!' yelled Martha.

Saru crushed her arms to her breasts and her face and stood rooted to the spot. She knew what was coming. Martha turned on her and started whipping her again with the stick, hitting her wrists and her face. I shouted, 'Stop it, Martha!' I jumped into the water, slapped Martha in the face and tried to wrench the stick from her. She turned on me. She gave me a blow in the face, here, above the eyes, and as I turned she cut me on the shoulder. Now I knew I could not stop her. I could not stop them and I could not stop it, whatever it was, and I started running for dear life. I leapt out of the water, grabbed my trousers and keys from the rock and bolted up the slope, towards the car. I stumbled and fell, stumbled and fell, clutching at bushes and clumps of grass to raise myself. I could hear them coming after me, Martha at the back and Saru in the middle, Saru behind me and in front of Martha, Saru wailing, 'Don't leave us here! Don't leave us here!'

I reached the car and fumbled with the keys, opened the door, pushed the key into the ignition, turned it and started reversing. They ran up over the cliff of earth, waving wildly at me to stop. Martha swung madly at the car with the stick, narrowly missing the wind-screen. I swerved away from them, turned round, narrowly missing a tree and accelerated up the dust track. When I was a safe distance away, I hit the brakes and glanced at the rear view mirror. I saw Saru fall, and Martha bending down to lift her onto her feet. I saw the be-seeching look on their faces, their feeble waving. I paused, wet and naked and bruised in the car, heart beating, engine running, my soggy trousers in a heap at my feet. I pushed the gear into reverse, then back into first. Then I stepped again on the accelerator, gently, and glanced again at the mirror. I saw them holding hands, watching me, two young naked bodies glittering in the sun, waiting for me to stop. I stepped harder on the accelerator and did not look back.

***

I'd ordered the waiter to bring him two beers and now, his story told, the young man took a swig, chewed at a piece of meat and stared into the fire. I could tell it was a story he had told many times. I looked at the scar above his eye, at the cuts on his hands and back which he bared to us; I listened to the sudden silence on his face and I knew this was not a story that he'd made up.

'So what do you think happened at the waterfall?' I prodded him, gently, cruelly, sipping at my second warming beer, unappetised by the meat, sober and undecided and still afraid to go home; warming my lonely unspeaking heart at the hearth of other people's stories.

'What do *I* think happened?' snapped the young man, taking another swig from his bottle. 'How should I know? What do *you* think happened? You tell us that! You've been standing there all night not saying a word.'

Play Your Cards Right

Always when he came to her flat he would fetch himself an ice-cold quart of beer from her fridge, pick up her phone and speak to various people – sometimes an uncle, sometimes a cousin. (She had learnt the Shona equivalents of uncle, cousin and aunt by now, and she was learning fast.) Sometimes slowly drumming the coffee table with his agile fingers, he would nod into the mouthpiece, but when the conversations stretched and wound, she observed a dark cloud creep over his smooth face. Then he would quench his despair with another pull at his glass while gripping the phone between his shoulder and jaw. Later she had learnt that his mother was incurably ill – languishing away somewhere on a farm or a village with some strange disease which her untried European mind could not contemplate. She had learnt too, with some sympathy, that half the calls he made were inquiring after his mother's health. That was why he could not spend his weekends with her, instead he drove to the country to see his sick parent.

She could not imagine what the old lady suffered from. He rarely explained – and when he did she could not reach a conclusive diagnosis. She was slowly realising that perhaps it was one of the many cases scientific medicine could never cure – a bizarre African case, one so often inextricably linked to spirits or witches… Perhaps if she understood Shona she would have made something of his clipped remarks. But with her, he only laughed and shrugged off her anxiety. Once or twice he let her speak to his relatives on the phone. She said two or three sentences – greetings – with a Shona word or two tacked in at the beginning or the end to show them that she was learning the language and, given time, she would learn their customs as well. And when he took the phone from her she heard their laughter booming from the other end of the country.

'Who is it, Timothy?'

He spoke on, while she pushed her steel-rimmed glasses up to the bridge of her nose, shuffled the cards and shifted fatly on her sofa.

'Was that cousin Tenda?'

'No, Uncle Peter.'

'Uncle Peter?'

'Yes, Uncle Peter, the hospital orderly. You spoke to him last week, remember?'

'Oh, Uncle Peter. But he sounded so much like Uncle Tenda.'

'You mean Cousin Tendai… '

'Oh, Cousin Tendai.'

'No. I was just discussing mother's condition with Uncle Peter. He thinks he knows somebody who could help her.'

'A doctor?'

'No. Somebody.'

He poured himself a fresh glass of beer and shuffled the cards with relish.

She was herself playing cards. Her blue-greenish eyes lit up with determination. Her fat hands firmed in the grip of her pack. Her back bent tightly over the table, her purple mouth quivered – the excitement buzzed.

But he too was shrewd, only a tiny little bit less than she was. For her, too, cards were a game of life and death, a ferocious contest. Together they would grapple for hours at the table.

'Come, Maria,' he yelled triumphantly, smashing a card on the table, 'Come!'

Tightly, like one caught in a vice, she drew a reply from her pack and smothered his short-lived victory. Bruised, nursing his defeated cards, he watched her closely as she rose, with a snooty little laugh, and like a prettily decorated circus elephant, moved seductively across the room to check the progress of the rice and mince. Often, when she won, he felt the urge to subdue her in his hot manly way. The razor-sharp vengeance with which they played each other, was almost childish, a sweet but cruel delight. (He adored her face, her neat mouth and her fresh smile. He cherished her plump body for its corpulence, and it made him feel good to be slim.)

Locked up in their battle, eating was always a nuisance. He ate his food in vigorous bursts, shoving the spoon into his mouth with one hand and throwing a card onto the table with the other. She took her time, a spoonful every minute or two, picking the finer slices of cheese with her fingers, sipping her beer with absorbed attention.

Hours later, after many hard-won games, when the cards had exhausted their minds and alcohol had quelled their ferocity, when his voice rode gently over the bubbling wave of her laughter, she would at last fling her cards onto the table, lift her dimpled arms languorously onto his shoulder and ask, Are you staying all night today Timothy?' She had a way of saying Timothy which drew out every syllable.

***

He always left her at two o'clock in the morning, because Tapiwa, his four-year-old daughter, would want to see him before he left for work. Aunt Chipo, a close relative who lived with them and looked after his little girl, grew anxious, if he did not return. She was, after all, his aunt and her role was to see that he did not do anything that might disgrace the family. And there were all the regular visitors – uncles, cousins, nephews – who lodged with him while they hunted for jobs: they felt deserted when he was away.

Maria saw Timothy as a typical African under siege from the extended family system. She didn't exactly dislike it, the system. It was different – she was simply lukewarm to its strong sense of communion. Its closeness made her shudder a little. The greed of the less gifted, the deprived, and the ruthless expectations they made on the few who had succeeded, who had benefited, made her pity Timothy. They all expected him to help. It was obligatory to feed them all, house them all, help them find jobs, soothe their griefs. If he did not do so, he would be a disgrace to his family and the wrath of his ancestors would descend on him, causing him to lose his job, his flat, and yes, all his little successes, little achievements. Yes, he would be reduced to a creature, crawling and ragged, he would be even worse off than they were.

Yet sometimes Maria could not but wonder why traditions still had such a strong grip on an emergent young black bureaucrat like Timothy. An assistant secretary in a government ministry, he was still fired with ideas about social change, though, like most bureaucrats, he endorsed the socialist ideology as long as it respected his position in the very structure whose destruction he preached. Sometimes too, when he spoke about culture, she felt he was a little flippant, that he had the strength of character to rid himself of the burden that was unnecessarily placed on his shoulders. He could shake himself free of his parasitic relatives if he really tried or wanted to, and there was really nothing to stop him spending half his nights with her.

He had brought her photographs of his daughter, once. Maria had instantly decided to love her. Tapiwa was so much like him – trimly built, fine featured, with a vibrant healthy skin and the same flashing smile that had conquered her. One day he would take her to his flat to meet all his people, when the domestic crises were over. She looked forward to the day they would drive down to the country to meet his mother. And then she would sit on the earthen floor of the grass-thatched huts, cook on an open fire and fetch buckets of water, barefoot, with the other women, from the well. Yes, she would show them that there was nothing special about being European. Only then would she feel herself to be in the real Africa.

Her own European past sickened her. She had battled all her life against the memories of her childhood in a small cramped house in a backyard street, and against the drunken rages of a tyrannical father who had cowered her mother into lifelong invalidity. Moulded into a rebel, she had defiantly braved the meaninglessness of being an only child in a cold loveless household; and later the suffocating feeling of being caught up in an endless rat race that seemed to lead nowhere. Getting her doctor's degree had not satisfied her and she had tried one thing after another until she had found herself in Africa's newest nation.

Four months now in the country, she had no real care in the world. There were no parents to nag her, no religion to haunt her, no letters to write if she didn't want to, nothing but the primeval desire to survive – as comfortably as possible, of course – and enjoy what pleasures her body afforded her. At the hospital she worked as hard as she could, but after hours she gave herself resolutely to reggae, drink, cards and Timothy.

Sometimes he brought his friends to her flat, and then she would give him her car keys, some money and a crate of empty bottles, and ask him to fetch some more beer from the bar down the road. They would sit for hours playing cards, rocking to the music, drinking into the early hours, even when it was a day in the middle of the week. As local hospitality required of her, she cooked meals for all those who came and allowed them to use her phone, though she winced when they scratched her records or, following Timothy's example, spoke for too long on the phone.

Her car was a fine old model Jaguar, and, like herself, roomy, comfortable and reliable. On two or three occasions she let him borrow it for a trip but when he brought it back one Monday morning, having clocked a thousand kilometres and lost the exhaust, she lost her temper. But she could not be really angry with him for long. He had a way of laughing it off and besides, she loved him too much.

Only a week after having the car repaired she bought his little girl an expensive set of toys.

'I'd like to give them to her myself,' she said. 'Why don't you bring her here one day and maybe we could take her to the park or some place else.'

'I'd have to talk to Aunt Chipo.'

'Really, Timothy?'

'Aunt Chipo's own child arrived yesterday to spend a few weeks with us. Tapiwa is keeping her company.'

'We could take the two of them out, and Aunt Chipo as well.'

'Yes, I suppose so.'

'We don't have to if you don't feel like it.'

'Give me time, Maria, Some day soon we'll sort things out...'

Some day, some day,' she muttered.

***

The cards were on the table when he arrived, but there was no beer in the fridge. And the telephone was locked.

He had found her door open and walked in, imagining her to be nearby, downstairs perhaps, in the laundry room. He eased himself onto a sofa, but almost instantly rose again to look through her collection of books. There were three new volumes, two on the plight of Moslem women and an English paperback criticising the monarchy. He wondered when she ever found time to read. After he'd left her at two in the morning? Perhaps she never slept. He picked out the book on Moslem women, skimmed the first few pages and abandoned it. The usual feminist stuff, he decided with amusement. His mind was constantly exhausted, he was not in the mood to read. He could not concentrate. Lately, he had felt that one day he would just break down. He looked again at the locked telephone, chewing his lips restlessly. He knew he had to be home early. His eyes swept the table tops for the key.

Damn it. Why had she locked the telephone today, of all days?

He picked up the scattered cards, shuffled them, flicked them onto the table. Maybe they would have the ritual game or two when she came. Changing the record on the stereo, he went into the kitchen to look for something to nibble and found a piece of old cheese. He was standing at the window, gazing at the car park below, when she came in with a cabbage.

'Hi babe.'

'Hi.'

'Been waiting ages for you. Had a good day at work?'

'So, so.' He sank again onto the sofa and started shuffling the cards. She slipped past him into the bathroom.

'Where's the key to the telephone, Maria?'

Only the roar of taps replied. He walked thoughtfully to the bath-room.

'I saw Tapiwa today,' she told him, sliding into the bath.

'You saw... '

'Tapiwa, your daughter.'

'Oh, did you?'

'I waited for her at the entrance to the block, and saw her coming down to buy an ice-cream. She looks so much like you.'

'You said so when you saw her photographs.'

'I talked to her.'

'Yes.'

'I said a few words to her in Shona. Showed off what you'd been teaching me. I also got to know she likes ice-cream.'

'She does.'

'We spoke for some minutes, then went up to your flat to see Aunt Chipo.'

'You did?'

'Yes. Tapiwa took me. I introduced myself.'

'Who else was there?'

'Cousin Tendai wasn't there. Uncle Peter wasn't there. Aunt Moira wasn't there. Nephew Elliot wasn't there. Nobody was there except Aunt Chipo and Tapiwa and me.'

She soaped herself vigorously and shampooed her hair.

'Aren't you going to ask what we talked about?'

'Tell me.'

'Aunt Chipo prepared some scones and tea. Her baking is so good. I asked her about the crochet-work in the room and she promised to teach me.'

'When is your first lesson with her?'

'Tomorrow evening. Was that your mother in the huge frame on the wall?'

'Yes.'

'She looked healthy and youthful.'

'That was before she fell ill.'

'What happened to your mother, Timothy?'

'You want to know? She had a stroke three years ago and lost her mind. She's a bit better now but relapses regularly. She's what you people would call a psychiatric case. Does that satisfy you?'

She rinsed her hair slowly, thoughtfully, dried herself, and wrapped her body gently in the big towel he handed her. She saw his forehead creasing as it sometimes did when he spoke on the telephone and she believed him. She believed him but fought hard not to relent to a strong feeling of pity.

'Tapiwa is such a clever girl, you know,' she resumed.

'Did she write you her name?'

'She did. And she read a few lines to me from a book. Do you teach her or does Aunt Chipo?'

'Aunt Chipo does.'

'Aunt Chipo is very good with her, very good.'

'Yes she is.'

'If all mothers were as good to their children the world would be a much happier place. What did you say happened to Tapiwa's mother?'

'I told you we separated and that I took custody of her.'

'Don't you think Tapiwa will grow into an aggressive young bureaucrat like you?'

'You think so?'

'Or perhaps she's going to be an inveterate liar like you?'

'What do you mean?'

'Your mother's illness is the only truth you have uttered in this flat. Everything else is a lie. Five months of lies which I eagerly lapped up.'

'What are you getting at?'

'Your culture was all you had to hide behind, wasn't it? And it worked wonders. All those non-existent uncles and aunts and cousins and nephews and nieces who were supposed to be driving you insane. All the ruthless traditions which bound you hand and foot.'

'So when did you turn detective?'

'I didn't have to investigate. Somewhere at the very back of my mind I've always suspected something was wrong.'

'Suspected what?'

'It all became clear when I went up to your flat.'

'Why did you do that?'

'I couldn't continue to let you think I didn't know, could I?'

'Know what? What are you talking about?'

'If you'd told me the truth I could have had a straight affair with you. God knows I've loved you enough. But now it's the monstrosity of your lies which has shocked me. How many others have you done this to before. How many other women have fed you, lent you their cars, their phones, their homes?'

'Done what?'

'Remember that weekend you brought back my car without the exhaust. You really hadn't been to see your mother, had you?'

'What makes you think that?'

'Later... you were so evasive when I asked how she was... So I did some arithmetic. It's only seven hundred kilometres to her home and back.'

'Who had I gone to see, then?'

'Another *murungu*. Another Maria Simpson. You've lots of us tucked away in different corners of the country, haven't you? Do we all give you our cars to do as you please? Do we all surrender our telephones, our booze, our bodies to you?'

'Stop it, Maria. If you didn't want me to...'

'I wanted you to. I wanted you. It's your lies, that's the problem. Your belief that you could lie for a straight five months and Chipo and I wouldn't know, wouldn't suspect, wouldn't find out!'

'What about you, Maria? You haven't been exactly an angel.'

'What did I do?'

'Those pills you stopped taking. You never thought I'd notice, did you? You thought you'd force a decision from me by having my baby. You'd caught me in your python-like grip and were swallowing me smoothly, slowly...'

'Yes, I wanted your baby. But I wasn't going to force you into anything. It wouldn't have made the slightest difference to my life. I'd simply look after the baby even if you deserted me, as I knew you would.'

'You played your cards so well, Maria. I was your guinea-pig all along.'

'At least I didn't have a husband tucked away that I called uncle; I wasn't cheating. You knew me through and through. And me... did I know anything about you? Do I **know** anything about you now?'

She was putting her clothes on. She had a steely strength which he had never realised, never imagined. He was afraid to touch her – for the first time since he had known her, she terrified him. And she was two years older than he was, and a doctor. Suddenly he felt clumsy and vulnerable, weak and helpless.

'What did you say to Chipo, Maria?' he asked in a hoarse voice.

'She understood in a way only a woman can understand. We're friends.'

Dazed, he followed her into the living room.

'Thank you for everything, Timothy. Be good to her.'

On his way out, he knocked over a side table. He bent to put it right and slunk out of the room. He wished for time to recollect, to pull his mind together. Something, the crooked root of his being, had been wrenched out and flung into the sun, discarded. He knew he would have to drink himself senseless before he took himself home to his wounded wife.

Maria stood at the window of her room and watched him go. She realised how futile her hope of understanding him had been. When he disappeared behind the darkened hedge she picked up the cards on the table and tore them up one by one. Afterwards, she flung herself onto the sofa and cried herself to sleep.

That night she dreamt about his disturbed mother.

Strays

The day they bought him from the white woman and let him out of his box, he ran round the house and could not be persuaded to eat. He assumed a look at once sour and forlorn and decided he would not be touched or approached. To be lifted and held was for him the height of human treachery – he would yelp and kick and wriggle himself out of the grip of intimacy, then plunge to the ground, gather himself together and bolt to a safe distance. No amount of whistling or cajoling could cheat him back into proximity, no fragrance of food could tempt him to stay on the enclosed veranda where rags and an old blanket had been piled up for his comfort. He would hold his distance for hours, sometimes even for a whole day – and then, perhaps in the morning, the milk left for him would be lapped up, the food nibbled, and sometimes, with luck, his plate would be licked clean.

***

A dog is a dog. The average African dog is a little less than that. The average African dog is a creature to be kicked, scolded and have missiles thrown at it – an inconvenient extra mouth that threatens precarious supplies in seasons of drought, or on rare munificent occasions such as Christmas, will efficiently devour the mounds of leftovers. For some women, the dog is still a handy convenience for quickly getting rid of the baby's steaming stool, a reliable voice that, shut out of doors, will warn off strangers, potential intruders and creatures of the night. It will shepherd cattle to the dip, hunt down hares and buck – a companion, tolerated, but kept hygienically at a distance. Before the advent of inoculation, it was a creature that survived on its own resilient biology, fighting off new and accustomed viruses while succumbing to disasters, physical and otherwise. Now don't say I'm cruel or heartless – I'm only telling you what I know and you can make of it what you will.

A European dog is more than a dog. (And European – even in these post-colonial times – is understood to mean white people as well as that small but resolute class of blacks who have padded their way up the social ladder with wads of money.) Not just 'the dog' or 'that dog', it is a member of the family with a personality, name, a kennel, a vetinary-aid card and, of course, a budget. It is bathed, shampooed, combed, patted, hugged, kissed, smiled at, loved, talked to, apologised and appealed to, argued and pleaded with, taken out for walks and pampered. It usually has a family tree, probably a place in its master's (or mistress's) will and is guaranteed funeral arrangements. When all is said and done, its status is on a par with that of the domestic worker in the household, the gardener or the maid. Such are the economics and the morality of the times.

A suburban African dog in an aspiring middle-class household is something between the two. While it probably benefits from the example of its white neighbours, it remains a household appendage. The status of domestic workers in African households is more blurred. Many are kith and kin and out of a communal fellowship the maid will probably live and eat with the family, so there can be no question of a separate budget for the animal. Humans unite in an outward display of kinship, so Kutu or Spot will have to make do with the leftovers, or leftovers enriched with a soup or meal supplement. Bathed or not bathed, trained or not trained, inoculated or not, this dog is a dog, promoted one notch above his village cousin. It will not be allowed in the house and while the children may play with it, it will not be allowed to lick them. It may be allowed to be friendly but it is not a friend, only a contracted worker hired to bark and keep the car and the precious colour television and video safe. Such are the economics of the other camp.

Now *this* dog, the one Sam and his wife bought from the white woman, the dog that ran off round the house and refused to eat, was a two-month-old puppy called Sango. He was an Alsatian cross with a traceable lineage and because he had been born in a Europ- no, a *white* household, he probably had elitist instincts. Sam was suspicious of the intimacy privileged people displayed towards their animals, seeing it as some kind of misanthropy. So Sango's status was already defined for him. He would be well fed and comfortable, but there would be no fuss. And at least he would be not just 'the dog', but 'Sango'.

But this dog, no, this Sango, complicated things with his elusiveness. Sango kept running away and ate sulkily of the milk, porridge and gruel they fed him.

'Well, what did you expect?' Ndai, Sam's wife, asked. 'He's a white dog,' Sam said begrudgingly 'or still thinks he is.'

'What's that got to do with anything? He's lonely and he just needs a mate.'

'Do you think we can support two dogs?'

'Most people with dogs have them in pairs. They say a pair of dogs is more efficient than one dog.' 'It's you who buys, the food.'

'You'll have to get him a kennel – one of those prefabricated wooden ones.'

'What's wrong with the blankets and rags on the veranda?'

'If you decide to keep a dog you'll have to look after him. He'll need bone meal, flea-powder, a bath tub and vaccination shots. And you'll have to start picking up his dirt in the mornings. We can't have the maid doing that. You know it's not good for a woman to be picking up dog dirt, any woman, especially a young unmarried woman like Moira. It will bring her bad luck. If people came here and saw us making her do this, they'd think ill of us. You'll have to pick it up yourself, or train him to use a pot or get a young man to do it. We need a gardener, anyway...'

***

Sam was perhaps what one would call the 'hard Mashona type'. The expression derived from a hardy, indigenous type of cattle noted for its rough-shod resilience. This type forages happily on the harsh scrub of the 'tribal trust lands', can put up with drought, tsetse flies and plagues of all sorts, for a time, anyway. He was a child of the village who had pulled himself up the social ladder through education. He was an architect by profession, having studied urban planning and architecture at university. He was newly married to Ndaizivei – a high school, home-economics teacher and they had one child, a two-year-old daughter, Natasha – her name reflecting his under-graduate romance with socialism. They had just moved into a house in one of the respectable suburbs of the city, having secured a loan from the firm of architects for whom Sam worked.

Why 'hard Mashona type'? Because, first, in spite of his achievements, he still preferred sadza and *derere* to the regular breakfast of tea, bread, eggs and cereal. Second, he preferred trotters, tripe, intestines and other offal to fillet steak and goulash. Third, he never openly displayed signs of affection towards his wife such as kissing, hugging or walking arm in arm or calling her 'honey', or 'sweetie' or 'darling' or 'dear' (though Ndai would have been the first to admit that this was more than well made up for in the bedroom). Fourth, he maintained his clipped, Catholic school accent (being a self-declared enemy of the tony 'nose-brigade' even though nearly all the people he dealt with at work were whites). Fifth, he preferred to drink, not in civilised hotels sitting on civilised stools, drinking at a civilised pace and nursing a civilised dialogue with civilised-looking strangers, but at bottle stores, straight from the bottle, layering off his beers with regular helpings of cowhead meat (nicknamed 'radiogram') and playing hide-and-seek with the patrol police. Sixth, because he preferred traditional music, rumba and *mbaquan'a* to the newfangled reggae, pop and rap. Etcetera, etcetera, etcetera.

He somehow thought that this slipshod environment would fortify him against the sanitised life of the suburbs, relieve the tension of those long, humanless hours at the drawing-boards of his office, and that it would help him retain his links with the common people.

Sometimes he felt a oneness with them which convinced him that he should have been an artist – a singer, or sculptor, or journalist, perhaps; and then he would smile to himself and dismiss the thought. Everyone feels like an artist when they've had a few drinks, he'd tell himself. Even a drunkard imagines himself reciting a poem, and feels the rhythm in his stagger.

***

After six months, Sango was a grown dog. Need had forced him to give up his discriminating taste and now he would gobble up his sadza and gruel as soon as they were placed in front of him. But he remained sly and distant, avoiding people. The only person he got close to was little Natasha, but that was only to snatch bread or bits of food from her, which sent her back into the house crying. Most times he sat or walked about in circles, looking bored.

'Maybe if there were more children here, Sango would feel more at home,' Ndai remarked.

'Is that your way of asking me to get you pregnant again?' Sam grinned, gesturing at her belly so that she clicked her tongue and slapped off his hands.

Some Africans moved into the house next door and planted maize and covo in the yard. Someone had rightly remarked you could always tell African yards from their maize and covo – the ploughing instinct certainly runs in our blood. We gladly rip trees and rocks out of our yards just to grow a few rows of mealies. Sam had been in his day a renowned cultivator of peanuts and tomatoes – but now there was not so much as a bed of wrinkled spinach in his expansive yard. Funny, what money and status can do to wholesome work ethics. The newcomers brought with them lots of children and two dogs, a male and a bitch. Their neighbours appeared friendly and Ndai suggested they introduce themselves formally, but Sam kept putting it off. And as soon as they had moved in, Sango migrated to their yard. He would not come home to eat and spent virtually all his time in the other yard, with his new-found friends. Disconcerted, Sam bought a chain, and went over to their new neighbours to fetch back his dog. After a few quick formalities, he went after Sango, chasing him round and round the house, trying to throw the chain over his neck. Eventually the man of the house helped him corner the dog on the veranda.

'Be careful with him,' the man warned as Sam, half triumphant, dragged the snarling, growling Sango home.

'So you went over and introduced yourself at last!' Ndai remarked as Sam chained the dog to a tree in front of the veranda. 'If it wasn't for Sango you wouldn't have done it.'

Sango wailed miserably through the night. At three in the morning, Ndai woke up and said, 'You'd better let him off.'

'You go and unchain him yourself,' Sam mumbled, irritably.

Ndai peered out into the darkness and then went back to bed. In the morning Sango was subdued and whining softly. He had wound the chain round and round the tree until it had left him only a few paces in which to move. His voice was hoarse, as if the chain was slowly strangling him.

'If the SPCA find you doing this they'll charge you,' said Ndai.

'What about the guard dogs that are chained overnight?'

'That's different, and they're *trained*.'

'Why can't Sango be trained?'

'If you've never bothered to teach him, you can't suddenly start with chains.'

'Shut up!' Sam wanted to swear, but he unchained the dog and let it off before he left for work. It slunk off, paced round the yard for a while, then settled down on the veranda. But when Sam returned from work, Sango had gone back next door.

'But how does he get out if the gate is locked?' Sam asked.

'He goes through a hole in the fence at the corner,' said little Natasha. 'I'll show you.'

Sam blocked off the hole in the fence with a huge stone. But when Sango found his exit route blocked, he dug a way under the fence. Each time his new tunnel was blocked, he would dig another.

'You'll have to put a durawall round the whole yard to keep him in,' Ndai said.

'First a kennel, now a durawall...'

'If you took him out for regular walks there would be no need for him to sneak out.'

'Or to have friends, eh?'

'I told you he needs a mate. What do you think he goes next door for?'

It turned out, to Sam's amazement, that the bitch next door was on heat. Sam returned from work one day and found Natasha peering through the low, thin hedge across to the neighbour's side. There was a loud, high-pitched wailing.

'Daddy, Daddy, come and see what Sango and Boxer are doing to Sheeba,' Natasha cried out, excitedly. 'Quick, Quick.'

'Come away,' Sam said, yanking her hand. 'Let's go and buy ice-cream.'

'Yeah!' said Natasha, racing to the car. Later, she said between licks of vanilla, 'But Daddy, why do Sango and Boxer do that to Sheeba?'

'I don't know, Tasha.'

'Do you think it hurts Sheeba, Daddy?'

'Just finish your ice-cream.'

When they got back home Sam said to Ndai, 'Why do you let Tasha stand at the fence and watch that?'

'What do you want us to do? Lock her up in the house? And what's so unusual about that? They're dogs.'

When Sheeba's heat cooled, Sango returned home and began to go out less often. He stopped tunnelling under the fence but developed a bold new way of running out through the gate. He seemed to know whenever somebody was going out, whenever he saw somebody wearing boots or carrying an umbrella or getting into the car, then he would slink up quietly from behind the rosebushes and the crockery and bolt for the gate. Before you could swing or shout at him he would be out, racing across the tarmac road into the grass and the trees of the adjacent farm. One day Sam picked up a stick, turned suddenly as Sango slunk up and he whipped and kicked the dog so hard that it fled back whimpering. From that day Sango grew afraid of Sam, and he did not dare to try to run away when he was at the gate. But when Ndai or Moira went to open the gate Sango would slink up, confident of his chance, and bolt out.

'Hit him!' Sam would shout, and Ndai or Moira would turn and swing or scoop or kick feebly and ineffectually at the open air – too late, and Sam would swear, 'You women!' And when Sango returned from his outing, perhaps an hour or two later and sat penitently at the gate, waiting to be let in, Sam would go out to the gate, walking and whistling as gently as he could and when he opened the gate and Sango rushed in he would land a mighty kick in Sango's belly and send the dog rolling in the dirt and scrambling up the driveway with nothing so much as a grunt that acknowledged his guilt. Once Sam hurt his ankle so badly from kicking the dog that he could not go to work for a week.

One day Sam came back from work and found a notice from the police saying he had to come to the police station to pay a fine because his dog did not have a licence and had lapsed on his vaccination shots.

'When did they come?' he asked Moira.

'In the morning,' the maid replied.

'How did they find him?'

'They were driving past and they saw him in the road and they stopped and asked, "Whose dog is this?" and I told them it's ours and they said, "Why do you let him out of the yard, don't you know he can get run over by a car or cause an accident?" and I told them the milkman had left the gate open. Then they said, "Does your dog have a licence?" and I kept quiet. And they said again, "Has your dog been vaccinated?" and again I kept quiet.

'They said, "You're the people spreading rabies," and they said I should give you this form.'

'Shoot!' said Sam.

He went straight to the police station, showed the form to the constable at the counter and said, 'I'd like to pay the fine.'

The constable gave him a long form to fill in. Sam looked at the form and said, 'Do I write my name or the name of the dog?'

The constable looked up at him and said nothing, so he wrote his name. Afterwards the constable copied out the information onto another form and into another book and it was a good thirty minutes before he finished and asked Sam to sign up on all the forms.

'What's the fine?'

'Four bucks,' the man said.

'Can I sign a cheque?'

The constable looked up again and said nothing, so Sam put the cheque-book back into his coat pocket and counted out the change on the counter.

'I'm two cents short,' said Sam. The constable looked at the money and said nothing. Sam turned his purse inside out and searched his pockets again till he found three cents in his back pockets. The constable took another ten minutes to register the payment and write out another receipt.

'Forty minutes of paperwork for a four-dollar fine,' Sam muttered recklessly as he pocketed the receipt, 'Some fund-raising.'

'*M'koma*, it doesn't matter who you are or what your cheques are worth,' the constable said, 'You must respect other people's jobs. And this is not the first time you've paid a fine, is it?'

Sam looked at the constable's face and began to think he had seen him somewhere before.

A few weeks after that, Sam was away in another town, working at his company's other branch when the phone rang in his hotel room. Ndai was at the other end of the line.

'Sango has been hit by a car,' she said.

'How did that happen?' Sam asked.

'How else – he was outside the yard and a car hit him.'

'Is he hurt?'

There was a pause.

'Is he dead?' Sam said.

'He's broken a leg and bruised his side badly.'

'He shouldn't have been out of the yard in the first place.'

'It's happened, it's happened, so stop talking about it.'

'Shoot! So what will you do?'

'You tell me. It's *your* dog. It's your dog and I've been telling you to get him vaccinated and to get him flea-powder and buy him a proper kennel and take him out for walks. I'm sick and tired of him shaking his fleas onto the veranda and dropping his dirt all over the yard. You should hear the way he was coughing last week. Just like somebody with TB. And yesterday he came back with a swollen jaw and bleeding cuts in his ears and was retching and eating grass.'

'You didn't give him rice and fish bones again, did you?'

'No! And now Natasha is coughing too. God knows what diseases that dog will bring my baby.'

'So what will you do?'

'What will I do? It's always me who has to do, do, do. And if I do anything you'll hang me for it. Come home and decide what to do about your dog. I've phoned a vet and he said they can put the leg in a case of plaster or put the dog down.'

'What?'

'Put the dog down. Kill him. He said I could bring him in first thing tomorrow. So what will it be?'

'You're the one there. You decide.'

She put the phone down abruptly and cut him off. The dog was coming between them, exposing the tension in their marriage. As with other minor household crises, the dog reflected the growing rift between them. He'd bought some flea-powder and given it a bath and he had tried a flea-collar but Ndai kept yapping and yapping. Okay, he had slipped up on the vaccination dates and the licence, but hadn't he tried to walk him up and down the road? Hadn't he bought a bone-meal supplement? She was using the dog to hit back at him and he responded by not responding and that only hurt Sango more. Every time they talked about the dog, he felt like plugging his ears and delaying whatever plans he had for the dog by another six months, until she stopped yapping.

He glared at the phone for ten minutes and then picked it up.

'Get the vet to put him in plaster and to look at his bruises. Get him to check his jaw and the cough, or whatever. I'll reimburse you when I come home.'

A few days later, he found Sango grounded in the garage, his whole right leg locked in plaster of paris. He was not to start limping about for another five weeks.

***

Now, where had he seen that constable before, Sam asked himself recalling the fine he had paid for the dog and the one occasion when he'd been drinking at a bottle store and had been bundled into the patrol raid truck, alongside hardened guzzlers of opaque beer and quaffers of *shake-shakes*, *kachasu* wrecks reeking of urine and sweat, sturdy imbibers of spirits and wine (pulled out of their sleek cars) and shrieking women, the vendors of eggs, *madora*, *ishwa* and other delicacies for the drinking palate. Men and women, old and young, married or single, fathers of homes, mistresses of cars, slim young women barely out of school, aching with high-heeled shoes and aglow with perfume, and great big wifely dames hardened with the misery of habit. He had secured his release after paying a $25 public-drinking fine.

The young constable had receipted his fine, once, at another station. Yes, it was him.

***

A fine is a fine and had to be paid, and if you were becoming a heavy drinker, as Sam was, you could expect regular fines.

A drunk is a drunk. There are many types of drunks, probably over a dozen species. In Sam's narrow habitat there are three prominent sub-species. The first is the average drunk, the religious imbiber who has to stop at the local bottle store every day, after work, to down three or four pints. He's probably a fast drinker, is most likely to be found drinking with a friend or two and will want to go home in time for the eight o'clock news. If there is anything to be done, it will have to be done by eight o'clock. When he gets home he will knock and his child will open the door for him. He might take home one or two pints and some potato crisps or candy for the children and will find the food still warm for him.

The second type of drunk might go to his drinking place straight after work or even go home to eat first. He will stay out longer, drink more, listen to some music, talk to people. His beer only goes down well if there is company, noise, music, women, crowds, the smell and heat of cigarette fumes. He might do a round of the bars, but in each of his haunts he has a special place, a corner that he likes. The waiters know him and if he runs short on a round they will say to him, 'Okay, bring it tomorrow.' When he begins drinking the alcohol takes him slowly and he might glance at his watch now and then. He sips out of habit, might even hate himself for it. He drinks because his hand feels the need to be clutching at something, because his throat needs to be swallowing something – if beer were water then he would be ordering bottle after bottle of H_2O. He feels a religious need to be sitting there, away from home, a need for this punishment of being stuck in this place, night after night, inflicting on himself the labour of drinking, of the noise, of the harsh and discordant poetry of the bars.

The third drunk is the worst. When bars close he will go to night-clubs and when nightclubs close he will go to shebeens and when the sun comes up he will rinse his face and creep home stoically for a change of clothes. If it's a Sunday morning, he might wait for the stores to open, then start on a fresh spree of drinking, trying to soak off all thoughts of his wounded, home-based wife.

***

Sam has a bit of each in him and yet is really none of these types. A mutant species. He does not fit into any neat category. He has no friends and no drinking mates and no specific haunts and yet he can create company for himself, company that only heightens his loneliness. His drinking times are defined, and yet within the pattern nothing is set, and he never ceases to be amazed by his own unpredictability. The moment he opens his gate and slinks out he feels a heavy weight of loneliness enfold him – he knows he needs friendship, love, but he is too stubborn to admit it. On the one hand, he spurns companionship and laughter, and on the other he craves them. He knows Ndai loves him but he aches for male companionship, male conviviality and camaraderie, the frisson of there being other women, the possibility or idea of freedom or a different kind of life, a different partner: he feels the ambivalence of belonging to a family and yet being unconstrained by it.

The clamour of all those drinking places rings in his head and time spins recklessly, hours squander themselves and the night slips by, so he wishes each day had a hundred hours and he didn't have to wake up with a headache in five hours' time to go to work, he wishes he didn't go to work and he'd really want to go now, but if he has company the bottles keep coming dangerously and he is stuck to this table, glued to this table, and he knows his only hope of rescue will be closing time when the band has stopped playing and is packing up and the waiters are ringing up the tills and counting the cash and saying no more service please, and he really has to go home now, stand up and leave this table and these women and these pints or else he'll be late again and he will be a late husband again and there will be another uneaten supper, damn it he hasn't eaten anything but he's now too full of beer to want to eat anything, damn it he didn't take the bolts out of the door and the keys are useless and he'll have to knock on the window and Ndai'll be mad to be woken up again to open the door for him, funny how she'll never complain when he's late and will only protest when he has to wake her up, but he knows her silence is her judgment but why has she let it go on until it has got to this why why why what is it Ndai can't give him or doesn't give him to make him want this, oh Ndai will she ever know will she ever **understand**, really he has to go now but this woman is looking at him in that inevitable way he only wanted to talk to her and her friend and he sat for an hour fighting off the idea of their presence, and then another hour pretending to ignore them, but yes tonight and last week and the week before he said to himself and next week and the week after and the next he'll say I'll go again and I'll only go for the noise and I'll sit and I'll drink for two hours and stand up and go straight out and go home but she talked to him asked for the time and he had told her and somehow now they have slipped and slid into conversation and now she is sitting there eying him and caressing her glass and waiting, caressing her cool quiet heat with her long thin fingers whimpering silently with her loud dark eyes and her slender neck whimpering for a leash and damn it she is small and still and tight and yawning widely bigly deeply secretly for him damn it why is it always long thin fingers he succumbs to, damn it why did God ever invent this thing called woman and whoever invented alcohol and bars and nightclubs and alleys and parks and the backseats of cars and booking houses and dark decrepit dungeons called houses in which humans called whores lived and the virus damn it the virus who invented the virus like being told you can't eat sadza and meat and *covo* any more the virus the virus why does it have to be this century and this decade and this year damn it all those statistics in the papers and those deaths in the news and waking up every morning saying am I am I, damn it all those droves of people sitting looking innocent would anybody ever learn damn it this weekly game of hide-and-seek with death and this big little woman caressing her cool quiet heat with her long thin fingers and tapping her long black purse with her long sharp nails and eying him with her condom mouth...

...damn it had all those ideals been reduced to this then, had his attack on elitism only dragged him deeper into his own scum, damn it but what was life without this danger to fill the emptiness...

***

Sometimes he wished he drank every day.

'That way I'd drink a few pints a day and wouldn't have to be out late,' he explained to Ndai, as if his worsening problem was something physiological that had to be planned for and explained and reviewed, 'The trouble is I starve myself through the week, and then when the weekend comes I over-indulge.'

'If you're a drunk you're a drunk, and that's it,' she said.

'Or perhaps I should make friends.'

'How can you need friends when you don't even talk to your neighbours?'

'Or play tennis.'

'The rackets are there in the wardrobes. And since when did you **mabhoi** start valuing sport?'

'Maybe I should go out and watch soccer...'

'We've heard that one so many times before.'

'Or even go to church with you.'

'You'd only be fooling yourself.'

He never went out on Fridays and by midday on Saturday he would be at the end of his tether, angry and irritable on a skimpy, rushed breakfast, angry with no one and nothing specific, exhausted already by having to race the clock, going to the bank and to the shops and doing all those wretched errands that crowd Saturday mornings into a series of miseries. As the afternoon progressed, he would look for something to fix up, listen to music, read magazines or play with Natasha, meandering in and out of and around the house till that invisible chain of irritation wound and knotted itself so tight around him that he felt he had to break free and go somewhere – anywhere, realising and fearing what he had known only too well and even hoped for, that there was yet again no domestic commitment to claim and save him from himself, no wedding and no relatives visiting and nobody sick in hospital to be checked up, nobody, nothing, nowhere, none, no one – he would have to get away, get away from the house, from this fenced enclosure and this clean, comfortable, safe, stifling building called home. He had to go out and go somewhere, anywhere, for this place to make sense, for him to be able to come back and make this place better, for him to come back exhausted and drained of all worry and full of love and gentleness and sentimentality so that he could play with Natasha and sit in his sofa and be served his food, for him to be missed as father and husband and to be wanted back home, for his demons to be quelled.

Natasha always knew he was about to leave whenever he put on his boots and cap.

'Take me to the park, Daddy,' she would say, or, 'I want to come with you.'

'It's not a place for children,' he would say.

'Why?'

'I'll bring you back an ice-cream.'

Sometimes she would cry. He never brought her the ice-cream because she would be asleep when he came back. She would be asleep and the street and the house would be dead and Sango would scowl and race up to sniff at the car and sniff at him and he would click his fingers to quieten him and drive him off and lock up and slink to the front door to do battle with the rattling locks. The house would be dead, but one morning she heard him come in and got up and said, 'Where were you, Daddy?'

He didn't answer and she said, 'Did you bring my ice-cream?'

'The shops were closed,' he said, keeping his voice low and leading her back to her bedroom.

Once he came back limping with a cut on his forehead and Natasha said, 'Did you kick Sango when you came in, Daddy?'

'No,' he said.

'Then how come you are limping? Last time you were limping it was because you had kicked Sango when he tried to get away.'

'I didn't kick him,' he said, and that was true. He had made a pact with Sango. It was almost as if he found his own sense of alienation mirrored in the dog's behaviour. Now when he found the dog outside the gate he quietly let him in. They understood each other, as if they were allies at some sport or as if they understood each other's constraints.

***

Then he returned with one of the back windows of the car smashed through and Natasha said, 'Who did it?'

'I don't know,' he said.

'But weren't you there when they did it?'

'No.'

Then somebody backed into his car and smashed the front so badly that it took the garage four weeks to fix it.

'Every time you go out something bad happens,' said Natasha. 'Why do you go out, Daddy?'

***

'You could just move out and go and live with her, whoever she is,' Ndai said to him one morning. There was no one and he said nothing.

'Or whoever they are,' she said, but again he said nothing.

'You dropped your rubbers in the bathroom and I put them on the window,' she said. 'You'd better save them because I'm going to ask you to use them.'

'You've sunk so low you'll have to use them,' she said.
But he said nothing.
And Sango slunk towards the gate.

Bramson

I never saw him much during the days when mother took him to help with the housework. He must have been fifteen or sixteen then. Three or four times a year, when we dutifully trooped down to the plothouse to spend the weekend with our parents, was his time off. He lived with a sister or relative, so we might run into him as he was leaving. Smiling shyly, he would open the gate to let our cars through, tuck his paper bag under his arm, give his half-salute greeting and then back off nervously, as if he needed to get out of our way: we, the children of the house. Occasionally we caught a glimpse of him wading among the eager chickens, replenishing the troughs or collecting eggs, plucking a bunch of rape or spinach or a pocketful of plums ever so gently for some visitor who had become the victim of our father's generosity.

'He's such a good boy, Bramson,' mother would enthuse, glad that after a lifetime of hard work, she could allow herself the modest indulgence of hiring a helper. 'He lives for his job and is no problem at all, unlike the girls who are always giving trouble.'

Those weekend visits now seem like rituals with which we intuitively sought to stave off tragedy. We'd left the little four-roomed house and switched to a bigger place, believing we were moving up the ladder of success. With our children fluttering like butterflies in and out of the rambling plothouse, we brothers, sisters, wives, in-laws, lazed on the verandah, gossiping in oblivious, unbathed languor, feasting recklessly on sausages, bread, scones, cake, steak, sweet potatoes, green mealies, *nyimo* and God knows what else mother had stocked up for just such an occasion; father beaming in the background, trying, as always, not to endanger the exchange with too many questions and not to bring out his budget book too soon; mother cooing contentedly among a forest of loving little arms, at the heart of our little tribe ... who would have guessed that in the midst of that apparent happiness and comfort, what we were going through or what awaited us?

Mother had had her premonitions, though. Decades before, when we were still children rushing off to school on bare cracked soles, scurrying in mindless poverty across the frost-bitten grass in thirst of success, she would wake up to announce her dreams. Fires, pythons and weird gatherings peopled her sleep; we grew afraid whenever she said, 'The dream I had last night...', so that she learnt to keep her nightmares to herself.

However, her fears were proved right when Rindai, soon after graduating from university and getting married, suffered an epileptic attack – the first of many – on the very night of his wedding. Just months later Kelvin dropped out of his first university year with schizophrenia. This was followed by a series of afflictions too bizarre to mention: ten bleak years of dogs dying, suicide attempts, bulbous tumours, sicknesses and strange visitations. The laughter died in our house, we cowered in uncertainty, impotent in our new-found material success, heads bent low, not knowing when some new terror would strike. We turned from bibles to herbs, consulting strange men and women who spoke to bones and prophets in promising robes of brilliant colour – bathing in unknown streams in the night, plunging deeper into the dark rituals of despair.

The laughter died in our house, yet no one died. And we had periods of reprieve that made us learn to grin back at the face of disaster.

Mother breathed tragedy. She scrambled to gather us up under her wings, squawking blindly at the eagles swooping on her brood. She fretted through every pregnancy, every trip abroad; journeyed to set camp wherever a crisis loomed. Suspending her own life, she lived for us, rebuking the forces that threatened us.

'Take me,' she pleaded. 'Take me and leave my children alone.'

***

Through sheer will-power, she must have succeeded in unseating the forces from their deep fastness or, at least, unsettling them. For they turned on her with a vengeance.

It started off with a relentless toothache. I drove three hundred kilometres to see her as soon as I put the phone down. Her face was swollen like a ball. Her eyes were deep and red and she would not speak. I could see she had endured many sleepless nights before breaking the news to us. Father threw himself into his cabbages and tomatoes, his face trembling as it had done when I brought Kelvin home from the psychiatric ward. Tawona sat grim-faced. She had taken mother to the hospital for X-rays. The results would be out in two days.

'And why didn't you take her to see specialists?' Vongai, belly looming in the glow of the bedside lamp, demanded on my return. I curled up speechless beside her.

She was brought to Harare by ambulance. The doctor said she had a malignant cancer and they would have to operate. When we went to see her in hospital, she reached out, threw her arms around Vongai and buried her head in the young woman's belly.

'It's going to be a boy,' mother said. 'It's going to be a boy and everything will be all right.'

She swung from hysteria to delirium to triumph. The pain was overwhelming. 'Everything is going to be all right,' she crooned. 'Nobody is going to suffer again. Not Rindai or Kelvin or Sharai or anybody. No more strange things will happen in our house. There's no need to worry. I've taken them on. Can't you see how strong they are? I've been battling with them for weeks. One by one I shall strangle them and quench their fires with this holy water the priest gave me. I am the prophet who has come to deliver our house from evil.'

They operated on her after a week. The cancer had spread all over her face. I saw the X-rays. The cancerous cells were in her skull eating at the bone, crooked cancerous roots snaking out from the terrible core. We took her home and waited for the wound to heal before she could begin radiotherapy. The cute, cheerful little nurses drew impressive diagrams of her head, like cross-sections of flowers in a biology textbook. For three months I drove her to the unit every morning so that they could burn the evil thing out. The therapy scorched her face, her tongue swelled. She could neither talk nor eat. She hung on for six months, dining on morphine, ampicillin, mouthwash and three spoonfuls of watery porridge a day.

***

Bramson must have smelt death settling on her. Bramson, the calf that she had nurtured, saw the streams of visitors come and go, and heard their frantic prayers. He saw men crush their hats to their chests and heard women click their tongues softly as they left that ill-fated bedroom. His young calf nose sniffed the air. The dank, sweet smell of rotting flesh and the devastation on her body terrified him. Or so I thought.

Taking only what was his, he packed his small suitcase and slipped into the night, quietly glad to breathe fresh air once more, ready to seek new pastures.

He came back months – perhaps a year – after the funeral. Father told us that he rescued him from the group of pilferers he was hanging out with – it is also said that he returned of his own accord, half-penitently to ask for his old job back. Anyhow he returned to the huge, now motherless, wifeless, womanless plothouse on whose fringes his presence had once tiptoed. With mother gone and all her children irrevocably wedded to their own homes, father installed Bramson in the house, gave him his own bedroom and not only made him cook, cleaner, book-keeper, seller of eggs, fruit and vegetables and collector of lodgers' rents, but companion and manager of his emaciated household. But even given that power, Bramson remained humble – quiet, industrious, honest – and none of us had reason to complain when we came to visit.

And with mother gone father launched into grand designs for the plothouse. With nobody to say, 'We've worked hard all our lives, my dear husband, and we must rest and be contented with the small comforts we've gained,' he extended the house, adding five new rooms. 'I'm doing it for you all, for the family, if it's the last thing I do,' he said.

The house became an obsession and we left him to it, imagining it would occupy his mind and ameliorate his loss but when the bills started hurting he turned on us with fierce accusations of neglect. 'Talk him out of it,' the women urged with feminine instinct, 'Why does he need to extend the house now that he is alone?' But with a new defiance, father soldiered on, brick by brick, as if the mere completion of the project was justification enough.

***

Vongai received the phone call and broke the news to me. In the morning as we raced across the country we hardly spoke. The news was relayed over the air every hour. There was a huge crowd in the yard when we drove in. The plothouse had been gutted by fire. Two sections of the wall had cracked. Half the roof had fallen in. Through the gaping holes of what had been windows we could see mountains of rubble on the blackened walls and floor. As we got out of the car, Vongai and Tawona started wailing.

'Shut up!' I hissed at them. 'What's there to cry about?' We stumbled towards the line of outstretched arms and the blur of faces scouring ours for marks of grief. We've done it again, I thought, angrily, struggling to look composed. Why does it always have to be us and our bizarre miseries that catch the attention of this whole, damned town?

Father sat on a sofa in the kitchen, surrounded by a crowd of neighbours and relatives, recounting what had happened. Although it was warm, he wore a jersey and a coat. He looked okay, but his hair was very white. I had not seen him in four months. His handshake was slow but firm and his look told us to be brave, at least in front of the neighbours. 'He was such a good boy, Bramson,' he resumed his narration once we had all settled down.

'He worked so well for my wife when she was alive. Being the young man that he was, he became frightened and left when he saw that she was dying. He was looking after me so well and not once did we exchange bad words. He ran this plot – did everything: cooking, washing, cleaning, selling vegetables and collecting the rent. Every Friday he would hand over the money to me and we would go through the books.' He paused, and as if the thought had just occurred to him said, 'He had become my paymaster.' But if there was a note of disbelief, or surprised recognition in his voice, it was not the moment to ask questions. Two or three of the neighbours stirred restlessly, almost suspiciously in their seats. My father resumed his tale. His voice had the hollow note of a tale too often told, at least to himself. 'Two months ago he brought home a pregnant girl and said, "Father, I want to marry this girl but my father and brothers are not helping me with the lobola, though they say they like her." And I asked, "Do you really want to marry her?" and he said "Yes."'

'Then I said, "Very well, Bramson, you know you don't earn much and a wife is very expensive, so you'll have to save up as much as you can. But she can stay here for a while, but because she's pregnant you have to go and show her to your parents and then take her to her own mother until she has her baby. We'll see what can be done once she has delivered."

'So the girl stayed six weeks and at the end of the month we arranged for Bramson's brother to take her home, since he happened to be making a trip to that area and Bramson was busy in the house and had not saved up enough for two bus tickets, and the girl's time was drawing near. We bought some groceries for his wife, Bramson and I, and she packed her things.

'Yesterday morning Bramson ironed the very clothes that I'm wearing and said, "Father, take off your jersey, so I can wash it," and I did. His wife made me breakfast and then knelt beside the sofa and said, "Baba, I am going now, but I will come back once I've had the baby" and I said, "Very well," and left them preparing to go to the bus station to meet with Bramson's brother. I had things to do in town.

'The next thing was that the police found me at Esau's hardware. They asked, "Do you know what has happened at your plot?" and I said "No," and they said, "Brace yourself," and I said, "But why?" and they said, "The boy who worked for you locked himself up in your house, set it on fire and hanged himself in the kitchen." I didn't believe them and I said, "What? You don't mean my Bramson? I was with him only a few hours ago." And they said, "Yes. But he's dead now and he has burnt your house down." And I said, "Take me to Bramson." I couldn't believe them. So they drove me to the mortuary and showed him to me and I shook him and said "Bramsonl Bramsonl" but they said, "He's dead, *mudhara*," and they showed me the note he had left and the long letters he had written to his father and brother...'

***

I saw my father sitting in his chair dazed and puzzled and yet perhaps almost enjoying being the focus of attention. I felt a charge of anger that we were being made responsible for not visiting him, for not taking care of him, for not monitoring his relationship with Bramson. I saw the neighbours' upturned faces. Nothing so exciting had happened in this small town for a long time. They were greedy to become part of the drama.

I saw my father in need naively allowing Bramson to become a companion, a companion that fed his vulnerable ego now that his childen had fled his nest. I saw that Bramson would never challenge him, never deny him. I saw that Bramson had replaced us.

I saw how I had failed my father, how we all must fail our fathers as times change, values change, and we are greedy for success in a new age. How we do not understand each other.

I saw Bramson hanging melodramatically in the kitchen. Had he hoped for more? Had he expected my father not only to treat him like a companion, a soft-spoken, uncritical companion, but to behave, in a time of his need, as if he were a companion.

Suicide requires forethought. While he ironed my father's shirt was he thinking about the rope he would tie round his neck?

Someone had a radio. It was muttering in the background. I saw him look at his watch. Another news bulletin. Perhaps there would be television cameras. I felt anger, and revulsion, and I wanted to stand up and shout: 'Go away. Go away. Leave us alone. Leave us to grieve alone! I heard the voices ...'

...We were there. Did you see us on the news? Such a tragedy. Bramson's tongue was hanging from his mouth. Poor old man. Building that house for his children. Not that they ever came to see him. Treated Bramson like a son. But as I always say it is a mistake to become too familiar with your servants. What could the old man do? He was lonely. Bramson was good to him. Perhaps the boy was possessed. To take his own life. Bewitched. That family is bewitched. The mother died of cancer. Such a growth. Her whole face eaten away. The son went mad. And those children ... but it'll do no good. The spirits are angry. They will not be appeased. The young, the educated, What can you expect?...

...I did not want to hear the voices. If Bramson had been there, I felt I would have killed him. I took a deep breath and tried to clear my mind. Bramson, why did you come back from wherever it was you went when you saw our mother was dying?

Why did you come back to kill yourself in our house, in our mother's kitchen? Were there not enough trees out there to carry the weight of your shame? If your life had become too heavy for you, why did you bring our house down with you? Or did you believe it was your house, because we kept out of your way? Even if you had stolen our mothers' dresses and our sisters' shoes and our blankets, did you think the fire would wipe away the evidence?

If it was something your brother said to you at the bus-stop, why take it out on us?

What about all those bitter words you wrote to your father and brother in those unposted letters – if you feared the drought and all those hungry mouths in the village, if your mother was sick in hospital and you had to pay lobola for the girl who had made herself pregnant by you – why did you lie? Why did your suicide note say that you were killing yourself because my father owed you $350?

If it was your dreams – the dreams you had of running amok and burning down your in-laws' huts – why did you pick on us? Was it because you knew people would say, 'Stranger things have happened in this house. This is nothing new?'

Why was your suitcase packed and ready, and the cash box empty when the fire-brigade axed down the door and found you dangling from the ceiling?

If you had wanted to spite Father for sending your girl off to the drought-stricken country, why didn't you just run? Did the fire get too big for you, get out of hand. Did you panic?

And why were you seen sprinting back from the bus station with your shirt tied round your waist, your chest dripping sweat, your eyes staring? What was driving you?

***

We are still waiting for Bramson's people. It's been five days now. We are waiting so that we can show his people this charred shell which was a house, this electric wire that tore down the ceiling board when the rope broke, the remains of the ladder, this box of matches. Nothing has been touched or moved.

Bramson is still in the mortuary; his eyes hard and cold as glass.

The gathering in our yard has dispersed; only a few relatives visit in the evenings. We're on our own, now.

The police have sent several messages to Bramson's father. The address was in Bramson's notebook. Record-keeping is something Bramson has meticulously adopted from our father. Rushinga. The police say the drought is very bad out there. The war in Mozambique has left people without cattle or goats. Bramson's old man is probably trying to sell off the last of his possessions to raise money to hire a van.

The old man will at least come, the police say. But we have heard too many stories of corpses rotting in village huts while people argue about restitution and people say it always begins with the aggrieved family refusing to come.

If they don't show up the convicts will bury the body, the police say. A docket for arson has been opened although the boy is dead. The police think it's true that Bramson stole mother's dresses and sold them. They think he set the house on fire to wipe out the evidence.

The police think father was a fool to trust the boy so much. They have read his letters and inspected father's scrupulously kept wage books where Bramson signed every month for his pay. They think, as we all do, that the suicide note is a cunning lie, perhaps an attempt to salvage something for his family, but under their tunics and their gleaming boots and their flashing watches and steel helmets the policemen are black Africans with totems and villages they come from and they know the word of a dead man cannot just be dismissed. They know suicide is not simply something that can be cut off a rafter and packed into a metal box.

We stay up very late into the night – three brothers, three sisters, one father, two wives and a brother-in-law. Only our brother Kelvin is not here – he is in some half-way house somewhere and nobody has discussed if or how or when we will let him know about this new tragedy. Bramson's death, like mother's, has afforded us precocious siblings, starved of spontaneity, the opportunity to vent our souls upon each other. We argue back and forth, fiercely and awkwardly, grilling each other, with reckless bitterness, till we glow like hearth-stones. We argue about everything – Kelvin whom we have dubiously sought to reform by banishing to the streets; father who has been ruined by ambition and trust; father's unspoken infidelity during mother's illness and his imprudence in wanting to remarry before settling matters with his in-laws; we squabble about the tombstone we still have to erect on mother's grave and the attendant ceremony which we, in our newfangled Christian folly, all secretly dread and don't know how to perform. We challenge father to prove that he did not indeed cheat Bramson of $350. Rindai entangles himself in vain hypotheses, I am hypocritical, Sharai introduces a note of laconic naiveté, Piwai parades her saintly airs and domestic martyrdom and Tawona stings us with a new smugness that has come with recent financial independence. Our wives smirk non-commitally in the fire-light. Young Tapera is quiet, taking it all in; the brother-in-law takes another swig from the *shake-shake* and, ploughing dangerously close to the truth, challenges father to reveal his plans to remarry.

The women sleep in what was the dining room – we men sleep in the kitchen. At any time the place might fall down on us, but we have exhausted ourselves and there is hardly any room for nightmares. We are done with herbs and bones. We're past that now. A boy called Bramson hanged himself in this kitchen and his body is in the mortuary – and so what? We challenge Bramson's ghost to disturb us during the night.

***

We are still waiting for Bramson's people. It's been a week now.

Last night I dreamt of Bramson running back, bare-chested, sweating and wild-eyed, from the bus station where he had accompanied his wife The extensions to the plothouse had been completed and the place was newly painted. Bramson's bulging suitcase and a huge cardboard box bound in a white rope stood on the veranda. Inside the house a strange but good-looking woman was fitting new curtains on the windows. Kelvin, head unkempt and cigarette jutting from his lips, came charging out of the house, exchanging angry words with the woman and strode, downcast and dejected, down the road. Mother, swollen-faced and wearing her church uniform lumbered out of the trees and, seeing Kelvin, shook her head. She waited at the gate of the extended house, gazing at the woman inside it. Bramson approached the gate, panting, and saw mother. He froze, the sweat dripping guiltily down his face.

'Come here, Bramson,' said mother ominously. 'Come right here, boy.'

In the soft breeze, the crowns of the pine trees overlooking our plothouse gently heaved.

Can we Talk

I hate the way you love medicines – the way you'll stuff yourself with painkillers, lozenges, cough syrup, antibiotics, lemon, sodium bicarbonate, mouthwash and honey just for a common cold. The way for you every sneeze is an allergy, every itch an infection, every pimple a cancer and every twitch a stroke. Your incredible faith in doctors – no, **specialists** – the way you will let them feel you, pamper you, cut you up like a guinea pig, punch you with their metal pricks, while gloating over you, and saying, yes, you said so yourself, you look like raw beef. The way they suck up your blood with their insatiable little tubes, and smirk as they sign the claim forms for some futile, umpteenth test. (God bless the Public Services Medical Aid Society!) But I know you think my grudge with the medical profession is academic. Perhaps it is, but I just happen to trust my instincts and I know your back has nothing to do with the fish you ate yesterday. What on earth does salmonella have to do with good old Sunday afternoon exhaustion? I thought you had done A-level biology? I hate the way you love to be ill, the way you court illness and gargle and cough and spit into the sink until you're really sick, the way you unashamedly declare yourself unwell to all and sundry and have your parents trundling over in their old Mazda to see you when you've scratched a knee and I'm not there when they come and Getty tells them I came home late again last night.

I hate the way you won't let me sink my hands into your hair or smother my face with your dreads and how you tie your head up in a doek or an old sock and wear a nightdress in bed, the way you heave off and curl away from my feet even if I've warmed them before climbing in beside you, the way you complain about my fingers chameleon-melion-melioning you – the way, some nights, when I've got you planned for all day, you'll roll yourself up in your miserable *puma* and edge off to the cliff of the bed. I just hate the way you say you hate my breath after drinking, even though you know I go through eight toothbrushes a year and the way you complain about the toothpaste when we go shopping and yet you yourself drink wine – yes, I've seen you lingering at the fridge at parties lately and don't think I don't notice your strange concoctions. And I just hate the way you sit up and watch TV until close-down and won't let me wake you up at seven on Sunday and then at a quarter past you will be up, thumping and squelching and huffing away at your silly exercises in the bathroom while I lie fuming in bed.

I loathe your ten-dollar hairdos, the way, against my sarcasm and threats, you yet again get your hair sewn up into painfully tight little rows, so close to your skin that your head looks like a ball or a snake, the way, even when you've got them, you tie your dreads up at the back like a nun and refuse to drop a deliciously aggressive curtain of hair over one eye. I should kill you for not wearing the clothes I buy you – you know and have admitted that the best clothes in your wardrobe are the ones I chose and bought for you – beautiful print cloths and styles I thirsted and starved to bring you from foreign lands – yet you insist on your brown skirts, blue blouses and black shoes when you are in your stubborn, funereal moods.

I could slaughter you for your boiled cabbage, cubed beef stews, boneless meat and fatless tripe. I think slim-you-slim has done you wonders – but you forget I'm a tribesboy raised to worship fatcooks and trotters and won't give in easily to your new-fangled crusade against cholesterol.

I could strangle you for your love of funerals, the way you are always going off to bury people I've never met and who never came to visit us and had no idea what we were going through, the way you'll put on your doek and wrap yourself up in your Zambia print cloth and be off on your mission of solidarity on just a chance phone call – as if to enlist your attendance at your own affair, the way you first look at the obituary and memorial column of the newspaper before reading the news and you are always the one to say who died when and where and of what and whose death anniversary it is.

I abhor the way you so easily hum along a tune you're only hearing for the first time, the way you applaud a stranger's success and bemoan a neighbour's woes.

I hate the way you assume I'll always do things the way I did them before – the way you always want me to be your regular man and refuse to understand my irony and open-endedness, my restless mind – how you forget to check the car doors or the oil and the radiator fuses and won't post my mail or take a vital message for me when I'm away. I hate the way your chest fills up and your voice trembles when I tell you off and the whole thing comes clattering down on us and I know we won't touch each other for a week and we argue about everything – money, relatives, plans, careers, responsibilities, egos and you can't even keep your voice down and the new maid and the kids will know we're at it again and you've always wanted them to gang up against me anyway and you sob and reach for your Bibles or sing hymns in my face or go off to the bathroom to mumble your prayers as if your God is an instant prescription for your headache.

I hate your silence and submissiveness, for I know it is a volcano that will one day erupt on me. I should crucify you for your other sins – your thrift, your envy. I know at the heart of your softness and humility is a hard secret nut of Capricorn ambitiousness, your straggler's distance is only a ploy to outpace yourself, to outpace me.

Yes, I hate you …

***

And *I* hate the way *you* never scrub your back and splash the bathroom floors and the walls when you take a bath, the way you leave hair all over the sink, the way you sit for hours in the toilet, blasting away like a motorbike for all the visitors to hear and then step out in front of me and elbow me out of your way, turning the mirror in my face, as if you needed to see your face as you wipe yourself up, littering the floor with twisted bits of tissue paper the baby might pick up.

I hate your baggy khakis and their misplaced creases, your unbuttoned shirts, your 'don't touch' turn-ups, knotted ties, wrinkled jackets and your obstinate mix-and-match style that make you so boyish. I hate your outdated Afro and the way you comb your hair so it sticks out like cat's whiskers and your shabby beard that needs a good cut. I hate the way you chew your fingernails right down to the skin and then claw me in bed. I hate the way you always savage your own body, tearing at your gums with your toothbrush and ripping out your hair in combful haste.

I hate the way you hate my relatives, the way you say you don't want them in your pockets and you don't want them to understand you, and you confuse them with your unpredictability. The way you'll do something nice and then when they warm up to you, suddenly back off. I just hate the way you conveniently choose to forget some of their names, the way you choose to hear what you want to hear when I talk about them, and when I remind you of something you look up with feigned surprise. I hate the way you dislike visiting my parents even if it's only a bag of potatoes that I have to collect and yet you know it is you who likes potatoes and you are always complaining about 'eating sadza and meat and veg everyday, sadza and meat and veg everyday'.

I hate the way you don't eat my food after I've spent the whole afternoon cooking and you stagger back home from your drinking spree and claw me with your ice-cold feet and crash out into a snore and I wonder how you've got home – how you ever managed to drive back, I wonder why you're killing yourself like this, why you're killing me like this, killing me with waiting for the phone to ring and the police to say you have smashed yourself into a tree or have been locked up or have been found with your head bashed in down an alley, wondering who or what it is that is keeping you out there so late, away from me, away from our kids. I hate the curt, sarcastic way you treat the children and think you can win them over with presents and surprise outings, thinking you can substitute financial responsibility for love.

I hate you for killing my love for you – killing my love, murdering my affection, slaughtering my feelings. You know once I would do anything for you – yes, anything. I would sing your name and was happy to be your slave and happy to let you mould me the way you wanted to but you kept drumming me with 'I'm not sentimental, I'm not sentimental' until I started hating buying you presents, hating buying you Christmas cards and birthday cards and Valentine cards – hating Christmas itself, and birthdays and things like that, until I was as unfeeling and unsentimental as you.

I hate the cruel way you use words, the silent way you uncannily absorb everything I say and then use it against me, the way you throw your whole self into a confrontation and turn your wit, humour and analogy into evil weapons used to crush me, the way you wriggle out of every argument and paint me up as the culprit. I loathe the way you bully and boss me about when we visit your relatives – believe me I was prepared to be your mother's own daughter and I became one, but you, you never so much as let my parents love you.

I hate the way we don't talk any more except when you are drunk – and then you nearly always taunt me, or when we're out at functions and you laugh and talk with people and I realize then there are windows to you that I can't see through, the way we've never really patched anything up and seem to teeter on the edge of reconciliation. I dread it every time we go on a long trip and you have to drive and you tense into a hard ball of anger and resentment and spite and you cut me off in front of the children – the road does something to you, the road and the open air and cramped car do something to you then and I know it's not me you are hitting at, it's not me and not even yourself you're flogging, but some demon that has dogged you, dogged your family in other forms.

I just hate the way you think you can contain me and my career, the way you think my life should be moulded by yours – the way you go on deluding yourself thinking I'm the same person I was ten years ago and that I will continue to put up with each of your emotional ambushes.

No *shaz*, I will not!

***

... and that night after your cousin's sumptuous wedding, out in the country, with the mountain jutting out like an axe-blade into moonlight and the valley snaking down from the hill of your father's household, through that land rich with intrigue and the bodies of your relatives, the air still with the breath of your ancestors and the fireflies serenading us and I belched the cow hooves that your mother cooked for me and the lager that your brother plied me with and the m'boora your sister served us and I giddily sneaked out with you to the lawn at the back of your mother's house and you took my hand and we soaped, scrubbed, rinsed, dried and embalmed each other and you were my mother, friend, wife, lover, mistress and we giggled and conspired and whispered, lying on a reed mat inches from your snoring parents and my head settled and stilled with the odour of the cow-dung floor and I rose to claim you and we had nothing, nothing, nothing to share but each other and I feasted on your salt and you on mine – that night you were supreme ...

***

We don't talk any more. So I've decided to write this. I know it is going to be a one-sided conversation but I will go ahead and talk, anyway. You have given yourself to God and I have surrendered myself to drink. I leave anguished, 3 a.m. notes pasted on the door for you, asking us to talk and I hear you talking to God in the bathroom in the morning, pleading with God, chiding God, warning God, quizzing God about why things have become like this. You leave square bits of paper with messages on the headboard before you go to work. You go to prayer-meetings on Tuesday nights, to women's church groups on Saturday afternoons, on Sundays you are a deacon and on Monday mornings you bank the church money. You read your Bible every night and every morning; you have Bible stories for our children thrice a week. You attend funerals, solidarity meetings and weddings. I think you mistake duty for love. I eavesdrop on you in your prayers. I try to find something personal, something by which God can definitely say, out of his book of a trillion souls, this is so-and-so and he or she needs such-and-such. Your prayers are general. You thank God for what we have been given – our lives and our careers and our children and the many blessings showered upon us. You ask for forgiveness and for guidance through another day. You pray passionately for the sick and the imprisoned, for relatives far away. I want to hear you say, 'Grab him, God. Bring him back. Let my husband go out there and drink three pints and come right back to me because I need him tonight.'

I think God is intelligent, creative and imaginative. Anybody who can invent the world, the universe, the human body, the mind, couples, sex, has to be. He can only be. He was. He is. I think prayers taken out of prayer books are too general, too vague. I think God must be able to say, 'This is a really good prayer – yes, I'll do what you want right away.' Or, 'What a sloppy prayer! Take it away and make it better!' But of course God enjoys a laugh now and then and often has to wait a bit, to leave things to sort themselves out. Already I can see you shaking your head and wincing and saying, '*Hamheno hako naMwari!*'* I hope it is not me who has intensified your faith through my waywardness. I hope that your faith is something you truly believe in. I have my own ideas about God – I think he is much more generous and understanding than you make him out to be. I am not fighting to win you back from God. We don't have to have the same beliefs. I think we should learn to live with each other's blasphemies.

I have so much to say, so I digress. And that is why I've so often wanted to wake you up three o'clock to say, 'Can we talk, please?' That is why after a function I always want to drag you somewhere – just the two of us – so that I can say, be my mistress tonight, come listen to my chaos and love me. Let my mind roll. It would be nice to sit with you at a bar somewhere. With the noise swirling around us. Right at the bar with the bottles glittering in front of us, spirits clam-

---

* God will take you up on this!

ouring, 'Sip us! Drink us!' Of course you don't take alcohol. You don't have to. But you can still come with me. Then, knowing I'm safe with you, I'll take eight pints and lead you through the caverns of my mind and if you're a good listener you might say, 'I didn't know you. I've been married to you for sixteen years but I really didn't know you.' You know what most men want? A sober wife at home and somebody drunk and vivacious to go out with. Now why can't one person, a wife, be both? I've gone out and seen elderly couples having a good time together and thought, what's the fuss? I think what most men want when they go drinking is a good listener. Not just a good listener, but a good arguer. And if the arguer can drink steadily with you and if she has a mind with caverns she can take you through slowly so much the better. I can't explain to you what alcohol does to my mind. You think it destroys me totally, brings out the worst in me. You have said you will one day tape me when I'm drunk and play the tape back to me when I'm sober. But tell me this – why do people say I'm nice when I am drunk? Are they lying to me? I think maybe I'm bad to you, or *seem* bad, because in the depths of my mind I know you don't want me in that state, so I might as well play bad and rebuke you and that's when it starts. Your friend Oripa once said to you, 'Why don't you drink a little with him so that you can get used to alcohol and to him?' Of course you steadfastly refused. And fifteen years ago that's a piece of advice I would have thrown right out of the window. You, my wife, drinking with me! But things change, my dear. I've mellowed so much you would not believe it. Doesn't it show? Am I still that God-fearing, father-respecting young man shackled by convention? Aren't I now more content to sit back and watch the world go by? Haven't I loosened up; don't I let you do what you want?

I digress. I talk alone. I badly need other souls on which to try out these ideas, other stones on which to grind the dubious grain of my conviction. Sometimes in the middle of the night I wake up with white-hot ideas and I reach out to scribble something down, and in the morning I read it and begin to doubt myself. I leave this desk and I walk out to once again immerse myself in life, to harvest the truth of other voices, to taste the wines of other experiences. When I am away from this tale I feel the conviction to go on with it, the confidence that I might pull this off and say something valuable, but I come back and I wax with the fear that you might not understand this, or that you might use it as an example of my diseased mind. I wane with the fear that perhaps I'm hopelessly lost, that I'm indeed beyond salvage. But let me try again.

I think I've forgotten what love is. I've grown suspicious of absolute feeling. I'd rather say, 'I like you so much', than 'I love you.' I think in my excursions I've learnt that friendship and openness and sharing are more sensible than love, that those who believe themselves to be secure in love need to be immunised against certain follies. I admit I have not always looked for love and friendship in the right places but I think there is more kindness, more understanding out there than one would believe. I have discovered that real insight and intelligence have less to do with background or class or education than what the cultural goalkeepers would have us believe. I think loving the souls of God's troubled children is commendable, but kindness without imagination is criminal. But then, I have forgotten what love is. Let me try again.

A certain man in his late thirties grew sick of love and went out searching for something better than love. He sought out women and said, 'Can you offer me something better than love?' and they looked at him and laughed and offered him their bodies. And he took them and said, 'Yes, but I want your souls as well,' and some of them understood him and laughed, and offered their souls. And he took the souls and said, 'Yes, but I want your minds as well,' and fewer still offered their minds. Then he said, 'I want your bodies, souls and minds altogether,' and a dozen of them said, 'Yes, you can have them.' Then he said, 'I want your collective bodies, souls and minds and let me pour alcohol and my music and talking and laughter and dancing over them,' and they said, 'All right.' Then he said, 'I want something more,' and they said, 'Like what?' and he said, 'Isn't there something more?' And they said, 'You need a girlfriend,' and he said, 'No, she couldn't take me,' and they said, 'You need a second wife,' and he said, 'No, she wouldn't be enough,' and they said, 'You have watched too many films,' and he said 'No,' and they said, 'There is nothing like that in our culture. You've read too many books,' and he said, 'Who told you that? Who told you that? I'm just being what I want to be and that has nothing to do with books or culture,' and they said, 'Maybe you need other men,' and he said, 'No. How dare you say that? I think women are more beautiful than men. I think a woman is the best thing God ever created. But I'm sick of women and drink and music,' and they said, 'Go back to your wife.' And the young man went back to his wife and she said, 'We've got to go to a marriage counsellor. We have to talk about this.' And he said, 'Go and make the appointments.' And she went and made the appointments and said, 'He wants to see you tomorrow. Alone.' And when the young man went to see the counsellor, the man said, 'I can understand your drinking. But why do you run away from home?' and he said, 'I want to be alone with my thoughts,' and the counsellor said, 'I know what's happening. This happened to me too. You are stressed. You are be-tween jobs. You are going through your mid-life crisis. Your family has gone through bitter times. But don't take it out on your wife.' When the young man returned home his wife said, 'What did the counsellor say?'

We did not talk. The counsellor packed us off with textbook assurances. He did a shoddy job. If anything, he needed counselling himself! We did not talk about him. You fiercely immersed yourself in your church manuals, assumed I was a changing man, prayed for me. I resorted deeper to drink. Heavy with the guilt of the knowledge of my problem, my knowledge of women, I shut up. We did not talk. We were both raised in the culture of not talking. Our parents talk-ed and we listened. Our teachers talked and we listened. The Bible talked and we listened. The Bible isolated us from our kith and kin, swept away the extended family, killed the traditional notion of the 'other'. Now we talk and our children listen. Our children shall talk and our children's children will listen. Now without parents or Bibles or teachers to talk down to me I have truly come unstuck. I have no one, nothing to *listen* to. I've chosen to live with the terrible satisfaction that no one shall say unto me, 'Thou shall not…' I've become a law unto myself, despite even you. Only I can change myself. But the Bible stays with you forever, even in the bars. The teachers step out of the shadows of the booking houses to say, 'Do you really want to do this?' And your parents visit you in your dreams, grunting, 'So what do you think you have achieved?' I was raised, like you, on manuals of the human heart from which tumbled beer bottles, snakes, half-naked women and burning cigarettes. Eve and the bright red apple. I was talkative and hospitable then and could entertain visitors of my age while my parents were away. One day when I was nine or ten an older cousin pointed at one such manual and said, 'Do you know you will be like this when you grow up?' and I said piously, 'No, I won't.' And he said, 'Yes, you will. Wait and see.' Later, while other boys were burning their fingers with cigarette stubs and scarring their tender lips with *kachasu,* I was sitting in the veranda of my mother's house, playing good boy. At school, while other boys were trying out liquor and vomiting seven-days' brew and cabbage and onion in the bathrooms, I was attending the Scripture Union; when my peers were already weaning themselves off their teens I was reading myself blind. Now I am the belated teenager, paying a hefty price for precociousness.

Now we talk and our children listen. You shut them up in the kitchen three nights a week to teach them the gospel truth. I watch Rumbidzai, already wise beyond her years, dutifully prepare the evening meal. I've tried to be her friend, written her intimate letters, striven to make her feel at home with me. But I realise even at sixteen, she can see through my flaws; that she is opening her tender heart to the world. I spy on Nyasha coyly doing her hair in her bedroom. At twelve, she is still my sweetheart. I see Kurai, the only son in our 'clan', happily kicking his football around the yard and I think, 'Will he carry our name?' Suppose something happens to him? I hear my children's accustomed squabbling and banter in the house and I realise how dispensable I am. I ache and groan with a hangover and struggle to the window to deliver a dry-throated instruction. Kurai races over and says, 'Yes, dad.' I think, will he know later when he grows up what I was going through? Will he forgive me? Will I ever be a role model for him? Will he appreciate that you and I survived, in spite of our incongruities?

We don't talk about these things but I think a lot about them.

My sisters held court with you. They said, 'We hear all is not well in your house. What's wrong, our wife?'

You habitually reported my 'crimes' to them. You reported my crimes to your sisters, to my brother, to my mother's cousin – my aunt, to your relatives, to our friends. My aunt called me up and said, 'Your father is dead. Your mother is dead. You have no mother but me. Tell me, what is happening?' I did not talk. My brother called me on the phone. He said, 'What is happening, *blaz?*' I said, 'Nothing.' I did not talk. I did not want to drag them into our affairs. I did not want any one of them to point fingers and say, 'You are the bad one,' or 'She is the bad one.' I wanted to contain our conflict. I did not want to sow the seeds of hatred. I knew my sisters were having conflicts with their spouses. I knew your sisters were having problems with their spouses. I knew our friends were fighting too. I knew my aunt had spent half her life sobbing secretly, darkly in her bedroom over a marital crime that was beyond words. I knew about my brother – I had rescued him several times after receiving tearful calls from his wife. Everybody has conflicts. If there were no conflicts life would be dead. The whole world is full of lonely, unspeaking couples. The whole world needs a symposium on talking. You vented your frustrations and ventilated them on my mother, sisters, my relatives, your relatives, our friends. For a decade I walked alone carrying the secret knowledge of your selfishness. For a decade I wanted to say to someone, 'She forces me to eat yellow maize meal,' or 'She does not even cook the spicy dishes I like, ' or 'She doesn't sew my clothes any more,' or 'I buy her material and she leaves it lying in the wardrobe for years,' or 'All her life she has bought me only a pair of shoes and a jersey,' or 'Whenever I have a drink she locks herself in the bathroom,' or 'She does not make me laugh.' I couldn't say, 'She doesn't let me think aloud,' or 'Whenever I argue with her she thinks I am condemning her,' or 'She does not let me be myself.'

I did not speak. And that was my terrible mistake. I hardened up with the bitter knowledge of your intolerance. And that made you harden up. We did not allow the frivolous intrusions of sisterly counsel to humour us back to our senses. I never said to you, 'Where is your aunt, so that I can talk to her about you?' We thought we were beyond tradition, that we were educated and sophisticated, that we could manage our own conflicts. Now look where we are.

Then I erupted. I could not hold it any longer.

I felt the confrontation coming. I yelled to your younger sister, 'When she is angry she sings hymns in my face!' I said to your older sister, 'Going to church doesn't make her a better person at all.' I rang up your mother and said, 'I don't think drinking is a crime.' And I drunkenly threw the tattered pink jersey and the pair of shoes you bought me over my aunt's elegant carpet and panted, 'This is all she's done for me – and she calls herself a professional!' I dragged in other irrelevances. I accused you of keeping secret bank accounts to support your parents. I accused you of pestering me with regular claims of being broke. I charged that you did not care about my work, that in your presence I could not think. I declared that I had no one to impress. I rang up my sisters and said, 'This is what you've wanted to hear all along...'

I was despicable. Losing my cool and stripping myself bare like that, after twelve years of stoical silence. Breaking my heroic silence. Seeking useless sympathies from people who gloated on my naked soul. People who themselves needed sympathy.

I have a lot to say. But I digress.

Perhaps I have realised how basic, how puny this life we are living is. Men running around in their suits and shoes and ties. Women in their costumes and lavish hairdos. Driving around in expensive cars. Living beyond their means. Going to work or to God-knows-what. Eating oily expensive lunches. Dialling the phones with their manicured nails. Laughing on the phones. Talking to mistresses, boyfriends, lovers. All trying to connect. Pouring out like herds, perfumed, lipsticked and powdered, from offices at five o'clock. To go to one-roomed dens. Cooking and eating and going to the toilet. Urinating, farting and defecating. Watching the same stupid soap operas on TV. Going to bed. Wanting somebody to hold, to love. Aha. Love. Sex? Companionship? Friendship? Or loneliness? Snoring and puffing all night. Waking up in the morning, white-smudged on the cheeks, to start again. The endless cycle. Living with this thing called life. Looking for love. Love?

I have tried simplicity. I've done away with shoes, ties, suits, jackets and God knows what else. I've done away with watches, calendars, diaries and appointments. I've done away with newspapers, radios, televisions and phones. I've done away with jobs, careers and hobbies. I've done away with friends and relatives. I've almost done away with *you*! I avoid the city centre. When I have to go there I slink in and out as fast as I can; I gasp like a stranger at the new buildings, at the walk-ways, at the one-way streets. I hear you say, 'So and so is dead' and it barely registers. I talk to a white-haired or a back-bent grandmother and they hardly remind me of my parents. I see a baby squirming in its mother's arms and am reminded of motions from another century. I see a laughing, rice-strewn bride and bridesmaid posing for photos with their troupe in the city park and I feel a deep pity. I meet a suited, cuffed, tied, shoed, brief-cased, barbered old friend and he eyes my sandals and T-shirt and khakis and asks the perennial question, 'So what are you doing now? So where are you now?'

So what are you doing now? Where are you now?

What is there to do? Where is there to be in this grubby little town? And I see you, my dear wife, clambering up the greasy ladder of success. I envy you your crowded life. You go to gym in the morning, spend the day quarrelling usefully with figures at work, drive your parents or sisters around, visit the sick, cook in the evenings, do the church stuff, study, sleep. What do you hope to do, my dear wife, when you reach the top?

I have so much to tell you, but I digress. Money or the *delusion* of financial success, my dear wife, is evil. I remember the days when we rented a little flat in Second Street and had a little old rickety VW Golf and you stood with the other women at the entrance to your office building, decked out in the dresses I had bought you and I gallantly picked you up and we went to fetch Rumbidzai from the crèche and we did the groceries together or you sent me to pick up the bread from that Greek man's bakery while you collected something from the pharmacy. We talked then, my dear. It wasn't the deep talk I'm aching for, the communion I have always missed, but we talked. We sat beside each other in the same car; I nearly ran over a dog or cat, a driver shouted rude things in my face, the car coughed and hiccupped at an intersection – we had to talk. We were man and wife. We did the budget together. We took little dawdling Rumbidzai for walks in the park and ate ice-cream. We ventured to the drive-in cinema on Saturday nights and ate chips and squabbled about film plots and I had five or six beers, secure in the knowledge that I would later gorge on you. And I even went to church with you on Sunday mornings, though I spent the two hours plotting or fantasising and I hated it when the preacher said to me, ' You tall man there, pray for us.' On Sunday afternoons we went to play tennis, and Rumbi would shriek and run after stray balls for us. And I always triumphed when I spent the weekend hunting for a part for the car and I found it and came back and told you, 'It's fixed!' And I relished the look on your face when I said, 'Someone is coming to fix the geyser,' or 'I'm putting up a prefab wall.' Or that day when I waved the papers in your face and bellowed, 'I got the mortgage!'

Now we cruise our different ways. I have no one to pick up from work or from school; I have no one to drive to school or to work in the morning. I haven't been to your office in years. I don't know you any more. I see you rushing off to work in the morning. You drive around in your new company car, wearing the costly outfits paid for by your company. I don't sneak any more into lady's shops to ask, 'Do you think this will fit my wife?' When I travel out of the country I don't squeeze my hairy, clumsy body into trim lady's dresses and prance in front of hotel room mirrors, smirking to myself, 'This will definitely fit *you*. Wait till you see this!' There is nobody for me to squeeze into women's dresses for. There is *no body* for me to please. Nobody to impress. And when you flung that wardrobeful of dresses into my face that morning after we spent the night quarrelling and you shouted, 'I don't want these any more! You can have them back!' you hurt me deeply, my dear. I had never been a talker to you but those dresses were my voice. I was the artist sketching you out, painting you up, exploring textures, fabrics and colours on you. When you threw those dresses at me you were telling me, 'Shut up!' Now we don't talk. We don't even quarrel. Sometimes we exchange ten syllables in twenty-four hours. Sometimes when we are asleep we curl up together between the sheets and wake up and separate. Your life is crowded and mine is empty. *Seemingly* empty. I've kicked down my ladders and deluded myself into thinking that I am in search of simplicity; but the vacuum is killing me. Yet I feel sorry for you, craving sophistication and clutching at the ladder of success, clutching and slipping, slipping and clutching, always trying to climb up. Climb up to where, my dear? I see you browse through the *Financial Gazette* and hear you say wistfully, 'So and so is doing well.' Doing well *at what* my dear? I am aware of the incongruous mix of your Christian humility and your craving for sophistication. I walk around and everywhere people want to shake my hand to congratulate me on the little success I've achieved. I ponder, how foolish of them to believe in success; if only they knew what a mess I am. But I badly need somebody to impress. Preferably *some body*. But I have no one to impress. Now I bring home a little of *my own* success and you don't give me that look of surprised appreciation. Now I am afraid to tell you about my successes and achievements. If I mention a cheque or trip or prize you immediately panic and take out your books to study. Yes, there was a time I was jealous of you, my dear, but I have mellowed. With the little that I have achieved I've become more liberal. Perhaps I've also become jaded. I see my friends in your field who work twelve hours a day and I think, 'Do you really want to join them? Be like them?' I think, my dear, one should be able to exist outside one's career; to step, with a little irony, beyond one's innermost ambitions and realise that life, living, is the ultimate career in existence.

I have so much to tell you. I ramble.

You remember Monica, the teacher.

The police called you rudely, boisterously and summoned you at seven in the evening and you went and asked Wilbert and Anna to drive you to the station. You cried all the way. Anna tried to comfort you. Wilbert only drove, in his quiet way. You got to the station and found us gone.

At the station they made us sit without our shoes, as exhibits. They said to me, 'Don't button your shirt.' I whispered to Monica, 'Don't tell them your real name,' but in her panic she did. They knew her husband who is in the justice department and had a grudge against him, so they decided to be real nasty and sent someone out to inform him. Monica went down on her knees in front of the sergeant and wept but it was of no use. And they saw my name on my ID and found our number in the directory and called you. No, my dear. I did not give them our number just to spite you, as you think. At the station they harassed us unnecessarily. We agreed to their charges, promptly signed the 'admission of guilt' forms and paid the fine, but they would not release us. Their plan was to have you arrive at the station and confront Monica, so that there would be a fight. Law-keepers! They taunted us. The sergeant said, 'But don't you two have a house to go to?' I know he would have let us go but the short one, the constable who had a grudge against Monica's husband, glared at her naked feet and said, 'If I was the one I would've taken her to the Lakeside Hotel for the night.' They taunted us, and we, innocents to the law, shocked by the mere fact of having been hauled to a police station, were terrified. The women constables said, 'Don't you have empty bottles in your car which we can borrow?' Monica naively replied, 'There's only a wine bottle...' and the slim, dark constable who kept giving me a sideways glance said, 'Lucky you, drinking wine in the afternoon.' We should have claimed our rights and said, 'We've signed admission forms and paid the fine. We didn't really break any law. You have to let us go.' But we let them continue, relieving their boredom on us. Eventually they did let us go.

We drove out of the police station and parked at the shops. Monica started crying and I held her hand and she said, 'What will my husband say?' We hatched plans to explain the incident, to show that we had been victimised, but when we turned them up-side-down and in-side-out we had a nasty feeling that the scheming was not water-tight. I drove Monica to their flat and left her at the corner of the road, with promises to see her the next evening. I drove straight home and the maid told me that the police had called and you had gone to Wilbert and Anna's house and I knew at once you must be on your way back from the station. I went and parked at the corner of Wilbert's street and sure enough Wilbert arrived.

'I'm in real trouble, Wilbert,' I said to him.

He tried to calm me down. He told me how you had cried in the car on the way to the station, how you had arrived just after we'd left, how the police, especially the women constables, had taunted you. He told me it was no use trying to lie, that I should tell the truth. So I came home and knocked on the door and you opened it and I said, 'Can we talk outside, in the car?'

I said, '*Sha*, I'm sorry,' and you sat there fighting off your tears and you eventually said, 'But why did you do it? I trusted you,' and I did not say anything and you said, 'What if the man sues you? Why did it have to be a married woman and why did you not have the decency to go some place else?'

We went into the house and you know how you held me that night, and what you did to me that night. It was as if you were out to prove to me that you had everything that this woman, Monica, had, and more. I think you were angry with me but you were sorry for me and afraid and shocked and you were claiming me back.

The next day in the evening I went to meet Monica. She was slow and sad, like someone who has been ill.

'He's very quiet about it,' she said. 'He has not told his relatives or friends. It's completely between us two and he wants to see what I will do. I think you must talk to him.'

'Talk to him?' I gasped. 'Do you think he wants to talk to me?'

'Phone him tomorrow morning.'

Next morning I went to a public booth and tried the number Monica gave me. It was a post-office number and they sent someone out to call him. He took a little while coming and I fidgeted with the coins and glanced at the queue behind me. A voice said, 'Hello,' and I said, 'Hello.'

I lamely introduced myself. 'I called to say I'm sorry about Monica…about what happened two days ago…'

He was quiet for two minutes, and I could hardly hear the sound of his breath. I heard the pain in his silence as he struggled with his feelings. I fed coins into the phone and waited. He spoke in an even voice that masked his bitterness. 'So you go around using your age and status and money to trick other people's wives,' he said. 'How old are you?'

I fed more coins into the phone.

'I said how old are you?' he repeated.

'Thirty-one…'

'She's only twenty-two,' he said. 'Why did you fall for her?'

I was taken aback by the question. I considered telling him that I had fallen for Monica because she was intelligent and vivacious and beautiful but thought that would be too brash. I stalled.

'Why did you fall for her?' he repeated. 'Because she looked available? Because she throws herself at any man who looks at her?'

I fed more money into the phone.

'Is that all you can do? Push coins into machines. Is that how you impressed her?'

I knew I should let him go on and vent his anger on me. I knew I should be quiet.

'What would you do if someone did that to your wife? Answer me. How long has this been going on? *Answer me!*'

'Three weeks,' I ventured.

'Three weeks, he says. Shamelessly.'

He was quiet again for two minutes. I could hear his pain as he struggled with his feelings, his bitterness. I could tell from the strategy that perhaps there was hope of getting through to him.

120

'And couldn't you have the decency to choose a better place than the roadside?'

I fed the phone. I wanted to say, *We weren't really doing anything...*, but clamped my mouth shut just in time.

'It's my fault,' I ventured. 'Please don't send her away.'

'Who are you to tell me that? Who are you to tell me what to do? Ah, you double-cross me and now you tell me what to do!'

'Please can I meet you and talk to you?'

'What would there be to talk about?'

'To explain...To...'

'You are thirty-one. You know how such matters are resolved.'

'Can we talk about this? Just the two of us, for Monica's sake?'

'I bet your wife has already forgiven you. And now all you need to do is to contain this nasty bit of work called Monica.'

'Can I meet you outside the post office tomorrow at nine?' I said, recklessly.

'Very well,' he said.

I put the phone down and staggered out of the booth, hardly noting the gestures of resentment from the impatient people in the queue.

Later that day, my dear wife, I met Monica to tell her about my telephone encounter with her husband.

'He's being quiet about it,' she said. 'He's deeply hurt and doesn't know what to do. But he's not letting me know that. He's not letting me know his plans, if he has any.'

'What do you think he wants from me?'

'Restitution.'

'Restitution?' I gaped. I had visions of High Court orders instructing me to sell half my property.

'What about you? Will he send you away?'

'Probably.'

'Do you think he will come to meet me tomorrow?'

'Try it.'

The next day I went to the post office. I thought it would be unwise of me to let him find me sitting in the car so I parked it near the shops and sat on a bench under the trees. I waited two hours for him but he didn't show up. I got one of the post office guys to go and look for him at his flat but the door was locked and there was no one at home.

That, my dear wife, is how the matter ended. I met Monica several times after that and she told me her husband had reported the matter to an older police friend who advised him to discuss the matter with his relatives. But by then so much time had passed that it was not easy to revisit the case.

That is how the matter ended, my dear wife. But the matter never really ended. Monica and her husband, my dear wife, were a young couple trapped in their own troubles and I only happened in on the scene. They quarrelled and patched it, patched it and quarrelled. I was a mere catalyst, a hapless channel, to their undoing. I've been saddled with the guilt of having been a home-breaker, but I was not a home-breaker as such. Monica was nineteen when she fell pregnant and she was in her first year at university. She had the baby and re-sumed her studies without a break. He was her first boyfriend, made her pregnant and became her husband. She had his baby but, like most people who have babies when they are green and aching for love and adventure, she wanted fun. She was young, beautiful and vul-nerable, but she wasn't totally innocent. He was youthful too, maybe only three or four years older than her, and you know men of that age are, sociologically speaking, a couple of years 'younger' than women of the same age bracket. He was no doubt magnanimous and gave her freedom and that was his undoing. He was not totally straight either – while she spent her Saturdays or Sundays out, he pretended to be home, sleeping, but he had a few things going on on the side.

That was Monica, my dear, and *Sha*, I'm really sorry. ...And why did I fall for her?

Monica loved books and talked about them with a passion. She had a terrific sense of humour. I instantly fell for her. She had read my books too and could say, 'Why did Godi or Farai or Benjamin do this on page so-and-so?' I relished her interest in my work. She was insightful and sexy and intelligent and had long fingers and an infectious laugh. We met in a literary forum. At first I thought I could have a platonic relationship with her, but when she confessed that her secret wish was to be an 'intelligent animal' I knew I was hooked. We spent days drinking brandy and roasting sausages and discussing, with increasing abandon, books and life. We were terrific together, but sometimes when we got carried away with talking we even forgot to be animals. She sent me a card with the picture of a zebra being mauled by several lions and captioned it: *Right now I feel like this poor zebra being torn right through the middle.*

That was Monica. She wasn't the 'slut' the policemen at the station made her out to be.

I could tell you more, about things that happened or very nearly happened right under your nose. I am scared about what I know about women. I live in potential fear of what I know about them, and what they know about me, and how my sordid life will one day burst into the open. I could tell you ghastly things about women. I am amazed how everything comes back to women. Women, women, women. I could tell you about kind women and cold women and cheerful women and simple women and evil women and intelligent women and women who cooked their brains, but I realise now that some things are simply unwritable. I keep getting to the rotten core at the heart of this story but here I am again, backing off. I realise now it is the synthesis of the experience that matters, and not the detail. Early in life, we men begin by relishing our sins and proudly cataloguing them but after a while we get bored. We weary of our own exploits, but we don't stop. Yes, we men are children. Yes, there is a polygamous streak in every one of us. Yes, six out of every ten of our thoughts are sex-related. Yes, half of us are probably sex maniacs. Yes, we drive around the avenues at night, flashing our headlights. Yes, we have girlfriends tucked away in high-density houses. Yes, we have secret children mothered by teenage girls. Yes, we can't feed ourselves. Yes, we don't care for the children that we spawn. Yes, we are irresponsible. Yes, we are rapists. Yes, we are wife-batterers. Yes, we spread AIDS. Yes, we don't last five years after our spouses die. Yes, we are weaker than women.

Yes, yes, yes.

So, I'm a sell-out, aren't I? Blaming men. Writing this unthinkable story. Shaming myself like this. I can see you shaking your head as you read this, Phillip, saying, 'What has become of the young man?' I can see you smirking, Jonah, and saying, 'Couldn't you write something else?' *Nhasi zvangu naWilbert!*[†] But I'm talking. It's good for me. I've been quiet for too long. I want to talk, talk, talk. Like Oliver Mtukudzi:

I want to talk, talk, talk
Ehee talk, talk
I want to talk, talk, talk
Ohoo talk, talk

It's cathartic. It's good to be able to say, 'I talked.' Talking is the basis of self-understanding. It's the basis of understanding others. Silence is too heavy. *Pamusoroi. Ndinoda kumbosasawo. Imi makambosasawo here? Munonyara kusasa? Nhai Phillip? Ko mupurisa uye wekuflat? Ndizvitaure? Nhai Jonah? Ko Mada? Nhai Wilbert? Ko sisi vaya veku Norton? Hamuna kumbopindawo mascene? Muri varume vakanaka nhai? Munonyara kutaura kunana'madam' venyu? Muchasvika kupi nekunyarara ikoko? Hamheno zvenyu.*[‡]

You know I have no friends. I see Wilbert once in two months and Phillip twice a year. Munashe, our neighbour, is a good man but we haven't yet clicked. Wilbert lives near enough. We've known each other for three decades now. We used to go picking *mazhanje* at school. I meet Phillip on the street and he says I must phone him. People meet on the street and say, 'Where are you hiding? You must phone me. You must come over to our house. Bring the Missus and the kids.' Nobody phones. Nobody comes over. Where do they hide?

In the early eighties, soon after independence, there would be par-

[†] I'm afraid of Wilbert.

[‡] Ladies and gentlemen, I want to talk. Do you ever talk? Are you too shy to talk? You, Phillip, what about that policewoman at the flat? I will say it aloud. You John, what about Mada? You Wilbert, what about that girl from Norton? Were you not involved with her? You are very nice husbands. You are too shy to talk in front of women. What are you going to achieve through shyness? It's up to you.

ties every week. I would phone Phillip or he would ring me and say, 'Where's the party this weekend?' People were always having parties. You could hop from one party to another to another in one night. There was excitement in the air. Independence. People getting new jobs. Moving into new houses. Getting married. Showing off. And everybody was young. Optimistic twenties. Now we are in our forties. We have children. We're tired of our jobs. Stuck with mortgages. Tired of our wives. Worn out by of our families. Plagued by ESAP and AIDS and bad government and fatigued political vision and traditions gone awry. We were born at the wrong end of the century. We are the AIDS generation. AIDS hit us where it hurts most. AIDS came and sneered at us: 'Now you can't eat *sadza* and *mabhonzo* and *covo*.[§] Now you can't!' And we pleaded, 'But how can we live without eating?' AIDS said, 'You think this is drop or syphilis? All right. Glut yourselves and see what happens.' Timothy Stamps rushed over and panted, 'Wait, wait! Here are some condoms.' Condoms. Condoms. We are the condom generation. The plastic generation. For some, it is no use. For others, it's too late. We are dying like flies. But we live on, clinging to the frayed edges of our lives with our pathetic claws. We live on, pretending things are okay.... We live on, hiding our despair behind the grin of masks. We are in our forties now. It's a dangerous age to be. We need something new and exciting. It's the age to tuck in your tail, stop dyeing your hair, go to church, find some sport or immerse yourself in the affairs of the school development association. Or drink yourself into a psychiatric ward. Or find a mistress. It's the age of divorce.

I need friends. I hate friends. I need friends and I hate them. I can't stand friends interfering too much with my life, but I ache for company.

I don't like men. They talk about football. They like to drive around in a raucous bunch. They want to go *kwa*Zindoga for trotters or *kwa*Mereki for a braai. Then off *kwa*Mukanya to dance. They are so predictable. They stand around the fire roasting meat and reciting the same shameless tired inconsequential jokes. I used to go *kwa*Mu-

§ Sadza with bone-meat and covo.

kanya regularly with Phillip. But now I don't go there because my sister's husband likes to go and I don't want to bump into him too often. You don't want to bump into your *mkwasha* too often in places like that. You never know who you or he will be with. It would be easier if we talked about it but we don't. I hate men. But women are no better, really. Women can be beautiful and intelligent and they can make a man open up and think and talk, but they sometimes have a curious way of thinking. They always think somebody else is out to get them. They can take you to task for one wrong word. They.... But let me not go into that, in case the gender brigade comes after me.

I hate men and women, but I hate to be lonely. So I go out and find a talking friend.

It's easy.

There are always lonely souls sitting at bar-counters, waiting to be chatted up. There are others at the side of the road, hailing lifts, but in truth waiting to be hijacked. There are people you know already, people dying for a visit, people you can seek out. If you walked into a crowded supermarket or an elevator and found a nice way to say, 'I'm lonely,' a dozen people would chime back, 'Me too!'

I make friends when I want to. But there is a big price for that. We talk a lot. I find out how old she is and where she went to school, who she lives with and where, her friends, and if she has a baby. Her totem, even. They always have babies. Everyone has babies these days. In our time if a girl had a baby people pointed at her and said, '*Akadhemejwa!* She was damaged. She has a baby.' Nobody paid much attention to an unmarried girl with a baby. She was a disgrace to her family, a curse to the mores of her people. But now it seems fashionable to have babies. Nobody worries about getting married any more. People don't marry just because they've given each other babies. In our time we fell in love, gave each other babies by mistake, and then got married. You know all my friends did that. Yours, too. S'manga. Nyasha. Dorothy. Albertina. Phillip. Wilbert. Simba. Tapiwa. Ourselves. We all bit the dust. *Another one bites the dust.* We all married too young. Before we really got to know the world. Now we are paying for it. We are trying, too late, to discover the world.

Neville survived the net. Neville was shrewd. He kept to his diesel engines and boilers. But now he is almost too old to marry. We didn't always give each other babies by mistake. Sometimes one partner, usually the girl, secretly decided to have the baby when things got difficult with her partner, to seal things up. Entrapment. I won't say much about that.

Anyway, I talk to my talking friend. I don't tell her what I do or who I am but she gets to know me fairly deeply. Names and details don't usually matter. I bare myself to her, indirectly, without committing my identity. I ply her with drink, with music, with laughter. We discuss childhood, schools, friendship, love, sex, girlfriends, boyfriends, wives, husbands, marriage, children, relatives, current events, myths and superstitions, dreams, apparitions, *njuzu,* African mermaids, political opinions, moralities, culture. Visions of Life and Death, of the Universe, of Good and Evil, of God. Even an eighteen-year-old can discuss these if you pitch the subject matter at the right level. Our conversation glitters with intensity; other people sit stiffly around us, eavesdropping, envying us, marvelling at the source of our inspiration. I try to find her soul. I burrow for her wit, her intelligence, her warmth. I make her laugh. We bandy about with dialects, with slang and our own verbal inventions. Everyone is witty and intelligent and funny if you allow them to be. I try to make up for my accustomed silences. I share myself with her. She becomes Woman and I become Man. But some friends build a wall of silence around themselves. They mistrust openness. They give you a low, sceptical, sideways glance that tells you that you have to give up. That you have to say your goodbyes.

It's easy meeting people. Every other person in the world is waiting to be met, to be talked to, to be found out, to be made friends with. But it's tough finding an eight-hour friend every week. Somebody really worth the trouble, that is. Somebody generous, intelligent, original. It's interesting because you never know what intelligence you will meet out there but the pattern of the encounters can get monotonous. The questions and answers can turn sour with repetition. People are the same, really. You land yourself a wealth of information that you don't know how to use. You start asking yourself, 'Is there nothing better than this? Is this all I'm cut out to do?' When you get taken for granted, and people's hands twitch for pints when they see you coming, you start asking yourself, 'Aren't I the one being abused?' It can get exhausting, degrading, humiliating.

I am an artist, my dear. Totally amoral. Selfish. Irresponsible. Impatient. Inconsiderate. Cunning. Sly. Cruel. Dirty. Despicable. Pathetic. Evil. Rotten. Mean.

All I have is my petty mind. And these flimsy pages to show for it. I'm jealous. Envious. Imbecilic. Insecure. Distrustful. Irritable. Covetous. Outrageous. Atrocious. Awful. Disgraceful. Notorious. Scandalous. Annoying. Dishonest. Ruthless. Unpredictable.

I'm an artist, my dear. I am not good enough to myself. I'm just not good enough. I'm never good enough. I'll never be good enough. I'm shy. Timid. Wistful. Pensive. Moody. Nostalgic. Sad. Suicidal. Ambitious. Proud. Pompous. You don't really know me. You'll never know me. Nobody knows me. I'm reckless. Extravagant. Egoistic. Loquacious. Gluttonous. Cannibalistic. Alcoholic. I'm an artist, my dear. I'm sick. I never knew I was sick. You never knew I'd be sick. I'm ulcerous. Myopic. Migrainous. Choleric. Diabetic. Asthmatic. Bronchitic. Epileptic. Syphilitic. Schizophrenic. Amnesiac. Cancerous.

I'm an artist, my dear.

I need tenderness, imagination, humour.

I'm an artist, my dear.

Can we talk?

Strange, but writing this is like having sex with you, my dear. Writing *is* a kind of sex. A ruthless, obsessive sex. Which is why writers and artists (male ones, as far as I know, that is) can never escape from women, or the idea of femininity or a sense of consummation. Now I'm not a woman and I don't know about women writers, so I'll leave it at that. Let me not say more in case the gender brigade comes after me again.

Writing this story, I've switched out my life for weeks. I've banished you, the children, relatives, *myself.* I've eaten, drunk, slept just so that I could reach the terrible orgasm of completing this story. The climax of this tale has eluded me many times. I now realise that perhaps this is not even an orgasmic narrative, nor even a languid confession. Some nights, sitting late in the cottage, at this desk, I've felt the strange welling up inside me, only to wane away. Some nights I've woken to reach out and clutch you. Or to ask you, 'Was I talking to myself?' I've felt my mind communing with yours with an unbearably intense clarity, and I have wanted to reach for pen and paper to jot something down. I've woken up two and half mornings a week to sit at this desk and try to put something down. Some mornings I've woken up, inspired, to bath and eat in frenzy, just like Kurai going to school. I have written a page a day, sometimes four or five paragraphs, and gone away for a drink. Writing this story, I have thought of you a lot. I have watched you sitting quietly on your sofa, or eating or sleeping or cooking in your slow quiet way, or taking our children to the doctor, or sewing and knitting, or studying at your desk and I have wanted to say, 'Yes, I think I love you. Yes, I've forgotten what love is, but I think I love you. I've forgotten what love is, but I don't think there could be anybody else.' I've wanted to say, 'Whatever it is inside me, love, lust, hatred, spite, imagination – it needs to be shared out because there is too much for me or for me and you alone.' There are times I've wanted to say, in between my forays to the cottage in the evenings, 'I'm writing about us. I'm writing about me talking to you, telling you about those things you've always wanted, silently, to ask.' In the middle of our silences, I have caught myself about to say, 'Wait till you read what I'm writing.'

This story has been a painful, delicious secret. I wonder now when you read this what you will think and what you will say to me, and whether we will talk. Will you forgive me for this? Is there anything new you will discover about me? Will we mend our relationship? Writing this story, I've suffered from electricity shutdowns, from angry unrelated phone calls in which one slippery word ruined my day, from my guilty conscience about sick or destitute relatives I did not visit, from old ugly family matters left unattended for too long,

fierce drinking sprees and hangovers that thrust into days. I've suffered from desperate Sunday afternoons when you and the children
went to church and I drove off alone in search of relief, in search of
people, in search of inspiration. I've never told you this, but Sunday
afternoons are my loneliest, most desperate days. Now I know what
your ready answer to that would be!

Writing this story, I've thought a lot about tenderness and imagination and simplicity and about how we are wasting our lives in
squabbling and silence and competition.

I have so much to tell you, but I digress.
I flee, my dear wife,
From the gilded wings of our hope,
          from long
       marinated weekends
blue chlorine fantasies & vanilla ice-cream
     VH1 classic symphonies framed in plasma-pretence
stocking(ed) lusts & se-ve-red duvet dreams
          soured domestic pacts larded
          with suspicion and regret
             & micro-waved futures.

And, always, the dreaded plastic smiles
Of your Anointed Brigades.

I flee from you, my butternut comrade
From Testament-trials
From you, from class
In search of Simplicity
(& Moreblessing & Nomatter & Prudence & Girly & Stha & Gau
 & Memo & Talent & Mati & Shayee & Mevi & Shupi & Trymore
 & Commonsense).
I scrounge for my childhood days
For my Hoffman Street forays
  pecking at desiccated loquat pips

Can we Talk

at the Greengrass –
Foraging for toy-car soft wires
Forbidden Benson & Hedges foil
And the vulgar cowboys blazing away at Mtapa Hall.
Of the tiny delights, which
I did not know then were ricochets of happiness.

In these bitter-bone-blighted streets
I savour the silences and slow motions:
A child mother – abandoned for Jozi, pulas and Harare North
Or *makorokoza¹* gold, sparkling *ngoda*** –
Draped in zambia-print-weave
Emblazoned with the fickle slogans of the season
Bosom heaving in black TRY ME T-shirt
Feeding her baby a *freezit*
And herself dining on a packet of *masawu*.
The superficial dust-calves of market women
Peddling fruit, fish, clothes, amulets, love potions
The wry banter of willing-wives
Lolling in sun/split gardens
             Hurry-less hairdressers
        Sipping sugared *maheu*
& crocheting secret melancholies
Baboon-bottomed boys booting flaccid plastic balls
In boorish streets
Racing ardent car tyres over ancient potholes.
The bustle of braai women and their hangover-curing smiles.
The marijuana mirth
And iron-grip ruin of stuttering Broncleer youth
Famishing for coins
And purpose.
And, always, the nonchalant, time-abiding stares
Of retrenched men quaffing scuds in the sheds.

¶   Gold panners who exploit disused mines.
**   diamonds

And these too I've loved –
The heat of ceilingless rooms
Red Cobra floor-polish and cement
The whiff of Protex soap, paraffin, candles, blankets,
sheets, paint & Shield perfume
Albums bursting with photographs
Mottoes on walls
The gentle twist of a bangled wrist
Turning *nyovhi* and *mabhonzo*
Curried road-runner chicken
Purpling in smoke-blackened pans:
'What would you like to eat?'

The yearned rusticity of out-of-town bottle stores
And Hi-Fi's blasting Olomide, Chimbetu, Mukanya, Chioniso,
Yondo Sister
Quiet lazy afternoons swishing with oblivious leaves
And the setting sun whispering, as always:
'Wait, wait, wait.'

***

I have so much to say, my dear, but I keep digressing. I realise now that I've been talking not just to you, but to other people, to myself. I wonder if I will get this story done.

There's a nightclub in Warren Park overlooking the Hills Cemetery. If you stop and turn round while climbing the stairs into the bar, your eyes will see right over the wall into the cemetery. In the moonlight the tombstones glitter like a forest of jewels. The nightclub is a small joint, but it is always full. When there is a disco the coloured lights flicker over into the graveyard. I think some of the younger ghosts in the graveyard are bothered by the noise. Perhaps some of the timid ghosts that want to exhibit themselves give up competing with the disco lights. But I don't suppose the older ghosts are bothered by the juxtaposition of life and death here – a nightclub right next to a graveyard, and they just say, 'Well, let them. We'll see.'

'It's a very peaceful place,' an old classmate, recently bereaved, explained to me one afternoon, braaiing some pork and sipping lager. Her name is Alice and she sat on the desk next to mine in Form 1; she would hiss my name whenever she could, making me nervous. But now she is a buxom sales rep and is married – well, she was, until her husband 'passed away', she discreetly explained, 'in a traffic accident'. Every other person dies in traffic accidents these days. We all know what the other half die of.

Alice and I are good friends. Sometimes she drives up in her car and finds me sitting alone in mine and she calls me over and buys me a pint. Our meetings are never arranged. We don't phone each other. Well, not any longer. Not since I phoned her once, when her husband was alive, and I was dying for a chat, and she said, 'Okay, but don't phone me again at home. It's all right with me but what will my husband say? You know men.' What will my husband say? What will my wife say? Friendship between married members of the opposite sex is something not easily allowed. We don't talk about it. We never talk.

Alice and I laugh about the past and we talk about the present. We nibble at the future. We are good friends. We talk. It's beautiful to say, I went to school with so and so and she's my friend and she's married and we drink together and talk and laugh – period. It takes years, maybe a lifetime, to get friends like that. Some people never have friends like that. I tell her my problems. She tells me hers. I say to her, 'No, Alice, don't do that to your in-laws,' or ask, 'But really, Alice, how does a woman go for a year without sex?' She can say to me, 'What? She's your wife and she's never bought you a beer?' or 'You just have to carry home a crate of beers, plant it in the bedroom and lock the door and say, 'My dear, this is how I am and you just have to accept me as I am.'

Sometimes when I am in a naughty mood I say to Alice, 'To think I spared you when you were hissing my name in class!'

But there I go again about Alice. I'm talking too much. Back to the graveyard story. It is said that some of the houses in Warren Park were built on old graves. So when the constructors had finished building, strange things started to happen. Stones were thrown at roofs in the night. Sometimes the occupants of the new houses woke up to find themselves sleeping on their beds *outside* the houses in the yard, surrounded by their belongings. And sometimes if you were walking on the street at night you would meet a tall man in a black suit who walked beside you, and if you greeted him he just grunted back at you. Then, when you got under the street light and you looked at him his eyes turned green, yes, *green*, and he veered back and vanished into the darkness.

Anyway, one night around nine o'clock I was driving out to Warren Park along the Bulawayo Road. A lady stopped me for a lift and she said she was going to Warren Park and I said okay. We started talking. Within minutes I had found out that she'd dropped out of school in Form 3, had a three-year-old son, had worked for a few weeks in a grocer's shop, was a VaChihera and like rumba music. As we turned off from the Bulawayo Road and approached Warren Park she asked me where I lived. I'd had a few beers and was in a jovial mood. I pointed out to Warren Hills Cemetery and, without turning my head or batting an eyelid, I said, 'My home is behind that wall. I died two years ago and was buried there. I occasionally come out when the moon is...' Before I could finish the sentence, the woman started grappling frantically with the door handle. I was afraid she might fall out, so I swerved off the road and hit the brakes. The moment the car screeched to a halt she jumped out and sprinted towards the houses. I jumped out and shouted after her, 'I'm not a ghost! I was only joking! You can come back!'

Not once did she turn back. She ran on and disappeared into the streets. I slowly drove on to the nightclub. I told the story to one or two people there. Later one night that same woman came up to where I was sitting and said, laughing, 'So you are the famous green ghost?' And we became friends.

No, that's morbid, you will say. But I talked about it. I could have told you about it, if you had let me.

Graveyards. Death. Alice's sizzling pork and corpses rotting away in expensive coffins deep in the earth a stone's throw away. Rumba blasting away from speakers in the nightclub and the quiet dirges of the burial processions a broken wall away.

Life. Death. Life.

'Do you know they are burying ten AIDS cases every day in this graveyard alone?' Alice asks. 'Very soon the place will be full.'

'Will you come to my funeral?' I've joked with Alice, and others.

'*Kutyei?*'[††] she laughs. 'I'll wrap myself with my Zambia and sit right next to your wife, crying, '*Iii, this man was sweet.*'

'And will you bring flowers to my grave?'

'Of course. But why are so obsessed with dying? Are you dying?'

'I don't know. But I don't think so. *Shah*, I've tried to be careful.'

'It's no longer just a matter of being careful.'

'What is it then?'

'Total abstinence.'

'Is that possible?'

'I've gone for a year now. I drink my booze, talk, or go dancing and then go to sleep.'

'You should teach me that.'

'It's easy.'

I've been to Warren Hills several times. Burying relatives, workmates, a few friends. You know I generally hate funerals and avoid them if I can. For the first twenty-five years of my life I never saw a dead body or attended a funeral, but in the last seven years I've buried a mother, a father and two brothers. It's frightening when you don't know what happens at funerals but it's dead easy once you know the procedure.

It's easy.

You get the news on the phone or from somebody face to face. You grab a chair, sit down, take a deep breath. You make a list of people to be informed, pick up the phone and the directory, make some calls. You leave messages, calm people down, try to sound solemn and experienced. You talk to a brother or sister, fix dates and places, discuss preliminary finances, assign duties. You throw some clothes,

---

†† Why not?

soap, toothpaste, Vaseline, a comb, a towel, into a bag. And something dark and solemn to wear. You marshal your party into a car, wave off gathered neighbours and friends, drive out slowly. Driving calms you. It gives you a chance to think, to plug loopholes. The women in the car – a wife, a sister, a cousin start singing. Your lips mumble the words – you have not been inside a church for a decade, but the words of the song come as naturally as breathing. You stop at a garage, refuel, buy Cokes, hit the road again. You finally arrive and see a piece of red cloth tied to the gate post and you hear the rattle of gourds and drums and the singing women and the reality of it hits you in the face. Women, always singing. Women, mothers with wombs. Women, wrapped up in Zambias, already cooking and serving. What would funerals be without women? You drive through the gate, into the yard, and wailing voices and arms throng you, tightly knit faces eager to be noticed surround you. You shake hands, embrace bodies and step aside to talk to people in charge. You drive out to buy mealie-meal, meat, bread, tea, milk, sugar. Someone brings a truckload of firewood, another one crates of drinks. If there is time you go out to the mortuary to see the body and if the body's face is smiling you feel okay, but if it's not, you're unnerved. If it's evening you have to wait for the hospital and district administrator's office to open in the morning.

It's easy.

You sit out the night at the fire with other men, sipping beers or scuds, talking gently, laughing even. If you're lucky you can sneak into your car to catch an hour or two of sleep. And at sunrise an elder knocks on your window and you rinse your face with a cup of water and off you go. You go to queue for the hospital doctor's post-mortem, to line up again to surrender the deceased's ID and passport and obtain a death certificate, to arrange for death benefits, if any, from the employer, seek out the burial policy, get the burial order, contract and pay the undertakers, hire buses, consult the priests for the church services, draw up programmes, order flowers, and all the time people stopping you to offer their condolences....

It's easy.

You can get it done in a day and a half if there are three separate parties of you, each working on a separate task, but if you are alone it could easily take you days. If it's the weekend you have to wait. That means more firewood, mealie-meal, meat, bread, milk, tea, sugar. More wailing, more handshakes and more embraces, more long- lost relatives, more nights at the fire. When it's all done, you rinse your face, put on a dark coat and a tie and sit on the bench at the church service and listen to the sermons and you join the queue to view the body. Then it's off to the cemetery in a convoy, tail lights flashing and horns sounding and you leave your cars in the shade of the pines and walk out to where the earth mound lies waiting, the fresh, lipless hole gaping for the body.

Earth to earth and dust to dust.

It's very quick at the cemetery.

The sermons are brief and the body is lowered into the warm, deep earth. You take a pinch of earth and sprinkle it at the head of the coffin and step out for the others. The undertakers remove their props, the shovellers attack the mound of earth with a vengeance, the women and the priests sing and rock to the rhythm, the hole is sealed and the mound of earth smoothed up. There are more speeches, the flowers are announced and laid and then it's done. Back to the cars and buses to more bread and tea and Cokes, to another night at the fire and more sadza and meat and cabbage. And if there is a thirsty bunch of you, you will sneak off to a nightclub and you will drink and dance yourselves silly to celebrate the burial, to forget. And at sunrise when you have had thirty minutes of sleep, another elder will knock on your window and you will drive out to the cemetery to check the new grave. And another will walk round and check the flowers and the new earth for any sinister footmarks or pokings and he will say, 'It's all right, isn't it?' and everyone will nod in assent and someone will say a prayer. Then it's back home again to a dimin- ished crowd, a trickling crowd, to pick up the pieces. To start clearing up. To return pots, drums, axes, dishes, plates. To assemble clothes, property, papers, bank books. To face debtors. To decide with elders on dates for the memorial service. To start discussing what to do with house, spouse and children, if any. If there are any people to discuss with. To start considering when to go back to your own houses, jobs, families, lives. To start *thinking* about the death.

'It's easy to die,' says Alice, licking the fat off her fingers and sipping her beer at the braai at the bar opposite Warren Hills Cemetery. 'It's the survivors who suffer most.'

'I am not afraid to die,' I tell her. 'I don't think there is anything I've missed in life. It's my children that I worry about.'

'There'll always be somebody to look after them. Whether or not this somebody is nice is the problem.'

'We were born in the wrong generation,' I say, offering her another beer. Two mini-clad teenagers recognise me and run up the stairs into the club, laughing.

'It's easy,' says Alice, chewing diligently at her pork. 'Just stick to your wife.'

'Do you think friends can meet in death…as ghosts…and love as ghosts?' I ask.

'You are a lonely man,' Alice says. 'You are a very lonely man.'

Printed in the United States
By Bookmasters